FIRE IN THE RECTORY

and two more John Nolan
detective novellas

Reviews for
FIRE IN THE RECTORY
and two more
John Nolan
detective novellas

"Engrossing ... One of Fire in the Rectory's strengths lies in its historical accuracy, which brings the era and its culture to life ... All the stories excel in a fine balance of whodunit, politics, cultural inspection, and a sense of 1900s America."
THE MIDWEST BOOK REVIEW

"Those who like an old-fashioned mystery with a dose of historical realism will enjoy these stories ... All three offer a vibrant sample of what life in New York City, just after the turn of the century, could offer."
THE BOOK REVIEW DIRECTORY

"Excellent ... Each tale has twists and turns I could never manage to predict. Was the fire an accident or arson? Is Mr. Hughes truly the sort of man he seems? If the most obvious suspect did indeed commit the murder, where is his weapon? I didn't even try to guess the answers to these questions but merely let the story take me along for the ride."
MANHATTAN BOOK REVIEW

Reviews for

THE DUTTON GIRL

**A novel and the first book
in this series of
John Nolan stories**

**Published by
Coffeetown Press of Seattle
in June of 2018**

"Deftly entertaining ... Certain to be an immediate and popular addition to both the personal reading list of dedicated mystery buffs and community library mystery/suspense collections."
THE MIDWEST BOOK REVIEW

"A classic whodunit ... The author does a fantastic job at intertwining historical facts through this story ... Progresses at a steady pace, giving just the right amount of clues and action to keep you entertained ... Interesting and believable."
READER VIEWS

"(John Nolan has) the quiet, self-possessed demeanor of a star detective with an understated talent for his craft and an appealing habit for being right when others are wrong. His slow, methodical investigation is fun to witness ... Competently crafted, with a bevy of suspicious characters and a pleasing variety of bum leads ... However, the most compelling aspect of the book is not who took a spoiled heiress or even Nolan himself, but, rather, how rich, poor, and working-class New Yorkers lived and interacted in the World War I era."
MANHATTAN BOOK REVIEW

FIRE IN THE RECTORY

and two more John Nolan detective novellas

by
STAN FREEMAN

HAMPSHIRE HOUSE PUBLISHING CO.
FLORENCE, MASS.

FIRE IN THE RECTORY
and two more John Nolan detective novellas

By Stan Freeman

Hampshire House Publishing Co.

www.hampshirehousepub.com

© 2019 by Stan Freeman

All photo illustrations are by the author.

Manufactured in the United States of America

ISBN: 978-0-9893333-9-9

JOHN NOLAN   **SHEENAGH NOLAN**

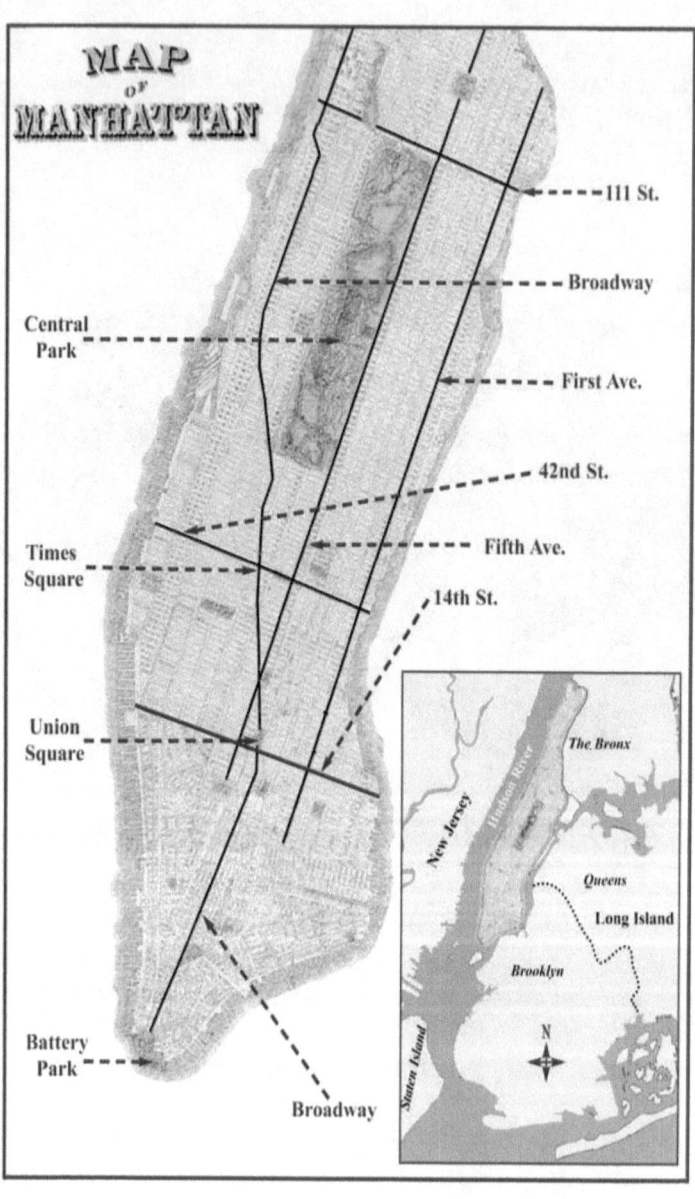

MAP
OF
MANHATTAN

111 St.

Broadway

Central
Park

First Ave.

42nd St.

Fifth Ave.

Times
Square

14th St.

Union
Square

The Bronx

New Jersey

Hudson River

Queens

Long Island

Brooklyn

Battery
Park

Staten Island

N

Broadway

Monsignor Broydick   *Catherine Broydick*

D. M. Stuyvesant

FIRE IN THE RECTORY

Interviewed in 1936 by the *New York Daily Mirror* about his long career as a private detective in the city, John Nolan was asked about the dark secrets in people's lives that his investigations must have uncovered and whether he regretted finding out some of the things he did.

"There was a case about twenty years ago in Brooklyn, but I'm not going to tell you which one. You hear some people say they have a secret they vow to take to their grave. Well, I'm one of them. The solution of this case burdened me with a terrible secret, but so far I've made good on my vow not to reveal it."

On a bitterly cold evening in late October 1915, a fire began suddenly in the library of the church rectory that adjoined St. Mary of the Assumption on Fulton Street in Brooklyn.

The rectory was brownstone and brick, but the blaze quickly climbed the flammable window drapes in the library. As it happened, several uniformed members of the neighborhood's Boys' Brigade Band were on their way to the weekly six o'clock practice in the church basement when they saw the flames filling the library windows and immediately ran to call in the alarm.

A horse-drawn pumper truck was the first to arrive

from the Central Avenue station. The deputy fire chief entered the rectory, saw that the flames had reached the library's pine rafters, and decided there was little hope of saving the building. So he ordered his hose team to concentrate its stream of water instead on the enclosed walkway that connected the rectory to the church.

He feared that if the blaze ever reached the church – with its oaken pews, wall tapestries, oil paintings, and $40,000 wood organ – that would be the end of St. Mary of the Assumption.

When the fire started, Nolan was at home – a four-room, thirty-dollar-a-month flat in a tenement a few blocks from the church – eating dinner with his wife, Sheenagh. Soon, he was vaguely aware of the sirens.

His telephone, the only private one in his building, rang during the dessert of peach pie.

"Is this John Nolan?"

"It is."

"The John Nolan who's the private detective?"

"It is."

"Well, this is luck. I didn't think you'd still be in your office this late. I'm calling from the New York Federated Insurance Company. Is your office still in Brooklyn, near Fulton Street?"

"It is." However, he had no office. He worked out of his home.

"Have you been hearing sirens tonight?"

"To be honest, you always hear sirens."

"I'm looking at a map of Brooklyn, and I think these sirens might be right in your neighborhood. Why I'm calling is could you do a job for us, and do it very quickly if you can. We'll pay generously."

—◆—

By eight o'clock that evening, when he got to the church, police barriers had been haphazardly erected on the sidewalk on Fulton Street. The crowd was already thinning, though.

The flames had been doused and surprisingly little smoke rose from the rectory, which, aside from one heavily charred corner, seemed largely untouched.

However, the frigid temperatures and the spray from the fire hoses had combined to coat much of the rectory in white crystals that glistened like diamonds under the electric street lights.

Nolan tightened his overcoat. It had been nearly two years since he arrived from Ireland and he still had not gotten used to the winters in the city. How did Americans stand it? He would ride the trolley and look around at others on the car and there would be nothing in their expression, no distress or despair, that said they were in any way suffering in the wretched cold. Yet, he did, and terribly so. He shivered even in the fall and spring.

He identified himself as an insurance detective to a fireman rolling up a hose and was directed to Deputy Fire Chief Swenson, just coming out the front door.

Nolan went over. "Sir, I represent Federated Insurance. We hold the policy."

"How'd that happen? Insurance companies don't hire new Irish."

Nolan winced at the insult. "It's just for this fire."

"Well, your company was lucky," the chief said, seemingly unaware of what he had said. "We thought we might lose the church too. We didn't even lose the rectory. Other than the rectory library, there wasn't so much damage as I thought there would be. Very lucky."

"In the morning, I'd like to come back and bring a photographer, if that's all right."

"Arrange it with the monsignor."

"Who's the monsignor?"

"Broydick. The Monsignor Broydick. He lost the great painting, you know."

"What painting is that?"

"You don't know about it? The valuable painting in the library? A Rembrandt, I think. If you hold the policy, that's the thing that's going to sting, I'll bet."

⁜

At that moment, Nolan was as highly regarded as any private detective in the city owing to a recent story in the *New York Herald.*

In early 1915, when he was twenty-seven and only a year off the boat from Ireland, he was working for fourteen dollars a week at his cousin's detective agency in Manhattan. He was able to solve a kidnapping case that had stumped New York City police detectives, and in a front page article at the time, the *Herald* had reported his role in it.

Three weeks prior to the fire, when editors of the *Herald*'s Sunday magazine section decided to do a story on "a day in the life of a private detective," their reporter went into the newspaper's files, found the kidnapping story, and contacted Nolan, who had recently opened his own agency. So it was a day in his life that was featured, the day being one in which he acted as a bodyguard for the famous stage actress Lillian Russell, who was appearing around Brooklyn in support of women's suffrage and to speak about the European war.

The story was so admiring ("Mr. Nolan could appear

on stage himself, such fine features does he possess."
"Mr. Nolan is a quiet and diligent detective whose sharp mind missed no detail in his effort to protect the renowned actress.") that in terms of reputation in the city, the Nolan Detective Bureau momentarily rivaled the famous Pinkerton National Detective Agency, which had offices across North America as well as thousands of agents.

In fact, Nolan had no other agents working for him.

The following morning, the crowd by the police barriers was larger than the night before. On their way to jobs in Manhattan via the elevated train, well-dressed men and women stopped briefly to examine the scene.

However, one group of women, some wearing winter coats over bathrobes, was standing at the barriers, apparently parishioners of the church. One was crying, her shoulders heaving, as Nolan approached. At first he thought the tears were of sadness, but listening to her, he realized they were of relief. The church was saved.

An elderly, silver-haired priest in a black cassock came to the barrier and the same woman kissed his hand.

"My first question was is the monsignor safe? Oh, my lord, is he safe?"

"I am, Mrs. Russo. I am."

Nolan waited until several of the women had a chance to kiss his hand. The monsignor, who Nolan judged to be nearly seventy, had what seemed to be a permanent kindly smile on his broad face. That made Nolan smile.

He tugged at the monsignor's sleeve.

"Sir, I'm from the insurance company, if you have a minute. I'm hoping I can look inside. And I have a photographer coming who'd like to take some photos."

"Goodness, I forgot there's insurance," he said, gesturing to Nolan to follow him past the barriers toward the rectory front door. "Everything has been so confused ... You look familiar. Have I seen you at St. Mary's?"

"Just occasionally."

"You have to do better than occasionally. God will be disappointed."

"It's my wife, Father. I came to New York a year before her and I would send her postcards with St. Patrick's Cathedral on them. So she fell in love with St. Patrick's and on most Sundays, we go over to Manhattan for their Mass."

They walked into the front hallway where small puddles of water were still on the hardwood floors and the strong smell of the fire was still in the air. The walls were heavily scorched. Then they entered the library, where the fire had been centered.

While the walls were intact – although most of the upper areas charred to a coal black – nearly everything else in the room was destroyed except the brick fireplace. The wooden mantle above it was thoroughly incinerated, and the bookcases that had stood to either side of it were now smoldering heaps of blackened, water-soaked bits of books and shelving on the floor.

"I was told the fire deputy first gave up on the rectory," the monsignor said. "He looked in and saw the flames had reached the ceiling beams, so he told his men to train their hoses on the walkway to the church instead." The monsignor shook his head. "It's unfortunate, and I don't mean to criticize, but if he'd only looked closely, he would have seen the beams were longleaf pine, which doesn't burn well because of all the resin in it. That's why they used it in the beams. He might have kept the fire from getting out into the hallway, if he'd gotten his men in this room right away."

He bent down to examine the debris. "Unfortunately, I had my collection of first edition books in here."

Nolan gave him a moment to himself, going out into the hallway to glance into other rooms away from the library – the monsignor's living quarters, a kitchen, a sitting room, and the housekeeper's apartment. The fire had not reached those rooms.

Nolan briefly stood at the library door, watching the monsignor pick silently through the charred books, shaking his head in dismay at each one he picked up.

Brought up in Tinryland in County Carlow, Ireland, Nolan had substantial experience with priests, since he was taught by them from an early age – and from an early age, he was quick to form judgments of them.

In his mind, they fell into a range. Those at one end were officious, stern, grim, quick to anger, and consumed with rules, those of God, the church, and the school. They were the ones to fear because of their habit of resorting to canes, straps, rulers, belts, and willow branches to punish the boys and girls who they determined had transgressed.

Then there were the priests at the other end of the range, those like the monsignor, kindly men who treated the boys and girls well.

Now he stepped back into the library. "Father, I was told you weren't home when the fire began."

"I'm very embarrassed by this, but I wasn't. My sister, who is my housekeeper, likes to go to motion pictures on

Wednesday night, and she couldn't find anyone to accompany her. So I did."

"Any idea how it started?"

"A fire department man was here earlier this morning and we talked this out. We always keep votive candles going on the side table in the library for visitors – and there are frequently visitors to the rectory during the week – and we figured that a candle may have toppled over onto one of the small rugs that we had in there. Or perhaps there was still a live fire in the fireplace – we'd had one going in the afternoon – that popped and shot out an ember onto a rug. This fire department man was satisfied with either of those two theories."

Nolan leaned down and carefully picked up two of the charred books, unidentifiable as to title. "Sir, I need to collect some of the debris for insurance purposes, if you don't mind."

"Go ahead. The books fall apart in your hands anyway. I found my Blake's *Gates of Paradise*. You could still read the cover, but it crumbled as I turned the pages."

Nolan reached into his vest pocket. "Also, sir. Here's my card, if you think of anything later that I should know."

Distractedly, the monsignor took it.

Nolan drew his wife's linen grocery bag from his overcoat pocket and put fragments of several books inside. Then, clearing material by the fireplace, he picked up what appeared to be a corner of a wooden frame, perhaps that of the Rembrandt, although the canvas itself was burnt away, and put it in the bag.

"I've been told something about a valuable painting, Father. Was that lost too?"

"Unfortunately, yes." He sighed. "It hung right here,

above the mantle and between the windows. As soon as the window drapes caught fire, that was the end of my beloved Raphael."

"Not a Rembrandt?"

"No, a Raphael." The monsignor appeared to wipe away a tear then. "My goodness, that had been in my family for one hundred years. It was one of the Madonnas of Raphael. I'm heart-stricken that it's gone, more so than losing my first editions ... which were in this bookcase here."

Again, the monsignor moved his shoe about in the charred rubble on the floor – the remains of his prized collection.

They were in a dim, upstairs office at the Brooklyn Fire Department building on Jay Street. The investigator for the Bureau of Fire Prevention, an Irishman named Walsh, perhaps forty, a considerable stomach, was at an ancient wooden desk covered with stacks of files. He was slowly going through the photographs taken at the rectory that morning. The developing chemicals were still wet on some of the prints. Nolan sat opposite him, his evidence bag in his lap.

Walsh, ruddy-faced and disagreeable, was another of those men who made Nolan smile. He was so reminiscent of his many uncles in Ireland. What also made Nolan smile was that Walsh was more evidence for the rule that one could tell the length of time an Irishman had been in America by his girth. The longer, the wider.

Nolan, at five-foot-nine and a trim one hundred and sixty-five pounds, had nevertheless gained twenty pounds since his arrival. Only part of that was due to the abundance of food in America. The rest resulted from Sheenagh's excellent cooking.

Nolan had slipped Walsh fifty cents and given him copies of the photographs to get him to meet with him.

"You ever investigate a fire before?" Walsh gruffly asked him.

"This is the first time."

"Then I'll make this educational for you, Mr. Nolan. Look here. What do you see?" Walsh handed him back one of the photos, a wide shot of the library.

"What do I see? Everything's burnt," Nolan said.

"Look at the base of the wall. The fire left it alone for the most part. The burning really starts about the height of your knee."

"There's a couple of spots where it made it to the floor."

"That's correct," Walsh said. "And what does that tell you?"

"What does it tell me? It doesn't tell me anything." Nolan stared at the two V-shaped scorch marks on the wall, ten feet apart, that began at the baseboards and widened out as they went higher.

"Well, if you're in the business I'm in, they tell you everything. They're the places where the fire spread from where it started on the floor to the wall and drapes and such. If you go on the theory that a candle fell, there would be only one V where the flames began their climb up the wallpaper and drapes. And the same if a fireplace ember shot out onto one of the rugs. There'd be just one V. But as you can see, there's two V's."

"The significance of which is what?"

"Mr. Nolan, that's arson you're looking at."

Nolan studied the photograph and slowly saw the logic. Then he sighed heavily. "This complicates things."

"My friend, life is always complicated."

As Walsh looked through the other photographs, he explained that there was often no lasting evidence of how a fire was set, that arsonists would sometimes stuff oily rags in sausage skins, then put a slow-burning fuse on them, even something made out of cotton yarn. Then they would light the fuses and leave. The fire might not start until fifteen minutes later.

"Half the arson fires in New York are set in Brooklyn," he said. "It's a popular hobby here."

"I want to show you one other thing," Nolan said, opening his evidence bag. He drew out the blackened piece of the frame. "The monsignor had a painting over the fireplace. Can you take a look at this? It's what's left of the frame, one of the corners."

He handed the charred, L-shaped piece, a half dozen inches on each side, across the desk. "The insurance company had a photograph taken of the painting because of its insured value – $28,000. What you have matches the frame in that photograph, the engraved pattern on the wood."

"Seems reasonable. The canvas, if that's what the painting was on, would be burned up, but the wood, which looks to be an oak, might not burn completely, especially if it fell off the wall and couldn't get oxygen or if the fire hoses finally got in there."

"Look at the back, though."

Walsh turned it over. "Seems reasonable also. The back was against the wall and it's not burned because the back wasn't getting the oxygen."

"Yes, but the canvas," Nolan said. "There's none left on the back."

Walsh sat very still as he examined the frame, back and front. Then he smiled. "You're right. And what does that tell you?"

"Now that I understand that someone set this fire, it tells me that the canvas was taken off the frame before the fire ever started."

"Very good, Mr. Nolan. You're learning."

"Did I miss dinner?" Nolan yelled out as he locked the front door behind him.

Beef stew. He drew in the wonderful aroma as he approached the kitchen door. Sheenagh was at the stove. When she turned, he looked to see if he could see any evidence of the baby, but she looked as slender as ever. They had learned only days before that she was likely pregnant. This would be their first, and everything about the pregnancy already seemed magical to him.

"I met the monsignor today," he said, kissing her cheek. "A nice man."

"Did you mention to him you've got a baby what's due in the spring? The baptism?"

"I didn't get a chance."

Disappointed, she turned back to the pot of stew, and he continued to embrace her. Life, to him, had reduced itself to a simple equation. His work, his wife, and now this child – they were what mattered in the final sum of things.

"And did you remember to mention me to the monsignor? I asked you to."

"I promise," he said. "Next time I see him."

Sheenagh's dream had been to have the rector at St.

Sheenagh at home

Patrick's Cathedral, Monsignor Lavelle, know her name, to greet her personally as they walked out of the Fifth Avenue church. However, the Sunday crowds were too large and the priests did not meet them at the door as they did in country churches in Ireland. So Sheenagh hoped to transfer her allegiance to St. Mary of the Assumption and to Monsignor Broydick now that her husband was acquainted with him.

"To have a priest in America speak my name like that, well, it would be like this country was the same country as Ireland. I would be home the moment he said my name. Do you understand that, John?"

"Of course," he said, but he really did not.

Nolan had learned that harmony in his marriage was maintained by not disagreeing with Sheenagh when she got hold of a certain kind of desire. To see an elephant at the Bronx Zoological Park, to taste a blintz, to attend an opera, to ride the Staten Island Ferry, to see the

Gutenberg Bible at the New York Public Library, to hear an American priest speak her name – when she got it in her mind that she had to have one of these things, he knew not to stand in her way.

They met in grammar school in Ireland, where six grades were taught in one room. When he was fifteen and she was eleven, Nolan began to feel a strange assurance that he and Sheenagh would one day marry. (When he told her of this, she stared at him in astonishment. "Of course we will," she said. "Didn't you know that?")

He arrived in America in early 1914 on his own, working at first for his cousin's detective agency. He saved enough money to bring her over a year later. They married the day after she stepped off the gangplank of the *SS Peterborough*, having dodged German U-boats in the crossing.

While America was not the dream that it had once seemed to him from the other side of the Atlantic, it was close enough. Brooklyn – and the rest of New York City – was thriving, as were the opportunities for detectives. And he made the most of his, earning a reputation as clever and honest. Still, the work was not constant and it paid only eight dollars a day.

"What did you learn about the fire?" she asked.

"Something very interesting."

In 1890, the tallest building in New York City was a church on lower Broadway. Now skyscrapers were seen throughout the southern end of Manhattan. The Woolworth Building, some sixty stories high, was the tallest building in the world when it opened in 1913.

The New York Federated Insurance Co. had its offices

in a new office building just blocks from the Woolworth Building, on John Street, taking up the first five floors. As Nolan asked around on each floor for the office of Mr. Stuyvesant, it became evident that the higher the floor, the higher the pay of its employees and the more extravagant the furnishings.

By the fifth floor, there were cut-glass chandeliers and oriental rugs in the hallway as he stepped off the elevator.

"I'm here to see D. M. Stuyvesant," he said to a receptionist. Behind her was a massive fish aquarium, filled with tropical fish that hardly moved. Beyond that was a long carpeted hallway of offices.

"See Mr. Stuyvesant about what?"

"About a fire in Brooklyn two nights ago."

"If you have a claim, go downstairs to claims. You take the elevator to the first floor. Just go out to the hallway and you'll find the elevator."

"Obviously I know where the elevator is. I wouldn't be here otherwise. It's not about a claim, though. I'm a detective."

"Police or private?"

"Private."

"Then why don't you just write Mr. Stuyvesant a letter. He's very busy."

"So am I. Mr. Stuyvesant called me, though, so go tell him I'm here." He said this curtly enough that, reluctantly, she went to find him.

Eventually, Nolan was directed down the hallway to a paneled conference room where six men were eating an early lunch at one end of a large, cherry wood table that could have sat thirty. It was only eleven o'clock. It looked to be roast beef and red potatoes served on fine china with glasses of beer. There were oil paintings, apparently portraits of company officials, on every wall.

Nolan stood in the doorway, waiting to be acknowledged. However, they kept talking as they ate, as if he were not even there. As best he could understand it, the discussion was about higher insurance rates on freighters now that German U-boats had resumed sinking so many in the Atlantic. Did the situation benefit the company? And the national referendum that was proposed on whether America should enter the war – would going to war benefit the company?

"Excuse me," Nolan finally said. "I'm looking for D. M. Stuyvesant. I was told to see him."

"Who're you?" asked a man about Nolan's age with a thin mustache and eyeglasses, apparently Stuyvesant. His voice was brusque.

"John Nolan, a private detective you hired."

"That I did?"

"That one of your people did. A Mr. Ganz."

"Is this about that church fire in Brooklyn?"

"Yes."

Stuyvesant, if that was who he was, wiped his mouth with his napkin and pushed a set of papers across the table to an older man who sat at the table's head. "St. Mary of the Assumption, sir. Insured for $220,000. This may be a problem. I can't find much in the policy to catch them on, but I'll keep digging into it."

The older man, whom Nolan took to be a higher-up man, studied the papers. The man who was apparently Stuyvesant turned to Nolan. "You. What do you know about this fire?"

"Quite a lot."

"So you're Irish?"

This caught Nolan off his guard. "Yes, I am."

"You know the dollar system yet?"

"Of course I know what a dollar is."

"Not what it is, but the value of the dollar. Can you judge the damage in terms of dollars? Not every Mick that steps off Ellis Island can comprehend the dollar since he still thinks in terms of his pound and shilling."

Nolan gritted his teeth, seeing what this was about. "Yes, I comprehend the value of a dollar."

Two of the other men farther down the table, not the higher-up man, snickered.

"What's your name again?" the man who was apparently Stuyvesant asked.

"John Nolan."

He turned to the others down the table. "I think the only reason this Mick got called by Ganz, who works the late desk, is because he lived within a few blocks from the church. Is that where you live, Mr. Nolan?"

Nolan only nodded.

"So your address recommended you, not your competence in judging damage, you see. So I ask you again – is there any chance you'll be able to give me a reliable estimate of the damage?"

Again, the two men farther down the table snickered. Nolan stepped closer to the table and leaned toward the man who was apparently Stuyvesant.

"You're paying me eight dollars a day so I'll be glad to stand here the rest of the afternoon listening to your remarks, sir, but if you want a report on this fire, why don't you stop asking questions like you're asking."

"And what are the questions like I'm asking?"

Nolan leaned in still closer, letting his jacket lapel fall away from his chest so that his revolver in its shoulder holster could be seen by Stuyvesant.

"Pretty much as stupid as the one you just asked." With this, the man finally seemed to be aware of Nolan's level of resentment.

"I'm, uh, I'm not sure we'll ever hire you again, Mr. Nolan." There was a shakiness to the man's voice, which pleased Nolan.

Now the older man, who had been studying the policy papers, stood. "Stuyvesant, leave this man alone. Sir, I'm very sorry. This is a major fire and we want to make sure we get competent information about it. What's your estimate of the damage, if you have one?"

"The fire was confined to one room in the rectory. It never reached the church. So you're not on the hook for too much, you'll be happy to hear. Mainly for the loss of one valuable painting. But there's something else. This might have been an arson fire set by someone to hide the theft of that painting."

Nolan slid a large envelope across the table so that it came to rest at the edge of the plate of the older man, who drew out Nolan's report. In silence, he began flipping through the typed pages and the dozen photographs.

"Very thorough ... Excellent summary ... Who took the pictures?"

"I hired a man. I have to charge for that. Time and expenses."

The older man continued to sort through the material. "Very good work. You said your name's John Nolan?"

"Yes, sir."

"From what I'm reading, we mainly owe for the personal items of the pastor, some books and this painting."

"A Raphael, so that's going to be the biggest expense."

"Who's Raphael?" asked a man farther down the table. "Why's he got only one name?"

"You're showing your ignorance," said another man farther down the table. "The Renaissance? Leonardo da Vinci? Raphael was nearly as big."

"Why one name, though?"

The older man closed the report and set it back on the table. "We will hire you again, Mr. Nolan. Very thorough indeed. Keep on it and let us know what you find regarding this arson business."

⁎

"But did he ever tell people what the value of the painting was?" Nolan asked.

The monsignor's sister and housekeeper, Catherine Broydick, a short, squat woman who he guessed was quite a bit younger than her brother, a decade or more, was preparing a chicken salad sandwich in the rectory's small kitchen. The monsignor was out delivering the last rites at a nearby hotel, Nolan had been told.

"You mean did the father say his painting is worth this many thousands of dollars? No. The father is not materially interested in money whatsoever."

She returned the chicken salad to the ice box. "Do you know that when our mother died – and this is twenty-four years ago – my brother gave every cent of his inheritance to the building fund for St. Mary's? He'd just been assigned the church and they were holding the Mass in an empty stable farther down Fulton Street while St. Mary's was being built. Every single cent went to the parish. I might as well have given mine away too. Instead, I invested it with a broker acquaintance who promised me great things. Then the panic of 1896 happened. I won't tell you the rest."

She handed Nolan the chicken salad sandwich.

"No, thank you," he said. "My wife just made me lunch."

She stood very still, the sandwich plate in her hand, staring at him. "What in God's name did you think I was doing here? I was making this for you. You should have stopped me before I got out the bread."

She said it with enough annoyance that he reached to take it, but she was already turning back to the counter to wrap it in newspaper.

Nolan regathered his thoughts. "Miss Broydick, you say he liked to invite people into the library to see the painting. Someone must have asked how much it was worth. He must have given some answer."

"What's this all about?"

"It's about insurance and how the fire started."

"The fire department will tell you how it started. Either a candle fell over or something flew out of the fireplace."

"That's not their current theory."

She turned and stared at him in a challenging way. "Yes, it is. The father told me it is."

"But they have a new theory that someone started the fire to cover up a robbery of the painting."

Miss Broydick laughed dismissively. "Oh, my lord. The stupid things people think." She angrily wagged her finger at Nolan. "The parishioners of St. Mary's – that anyone could think one of them stole the painting and tried to burn down the church ... Why it's ... it's the thought of someone who's an atheist. Are you an atheist, Mr. Nolan?"

"No, but that doesn't change the fact that the fire department is convinced this was a robbery and arson. Now, could you please answer the question? Did the monsignor ever mention a figure for the value of the painting?"

They stared at each other, a silent tug of war that Nolan's stern, unrelenting gaze finally won.

"The father didn't even know the value. He only guessed, but yes, once in a while, he would mention a figure, just trying to impress these people of how important the Raphael was."

"And what figure was that?"

"Go ask him. I don't know."

"But you just said you heard him mention a figure. What figure did you hear him —"

She shook her head in exasperation. "All right, Mr. Nolan. Once I heard him say $300,000. There. You've got your answer. That's all I'm going to tell you."

However, the monsignor's sister told him one more thing – where the monsignor had gone to give the last rites. The St. Vincent Hotel, several blocks down on Fulton Street.

Nolan saw the motor truck of the fire department rescue squad parked outside the hotel.

On the second floor, the monsignor was standing in a solemn crowd of men while the rescue squad was at work nearby at the elevator shaft. The car was stuck between floors and a short pair of legs could be seen dangling from just inside the top of the elevator door. Sparks from an oxy-acetylene blowpipe were showering the hallway.

Nolan learned a thirteen-year-old boy was operating the elevator when it slipped its brakes, wedging him between floors, and now the rescue squad was trying to cut him out.

Spotting Nolan, the monsignor extended his hand. "How long have you been standing there?"

"Not long, Father. I hoped we could talk a minute, but it looks like you're busy."

"I've done all I can. He may already be dead, though. So please, go ahead."

The monsignor led Nolan farther down the hall, away from the noise.

"It's just, uh, some new evidence has come out about the fire," Nolan said. "It points to something else going on. It looks like the fire was set by someone to hide a robbery, the robbery of your painting."

The monsignor looked away, toward the crowd up the hallway. He said nothing.

"Sir?"

"I heard you."

"What do you think?"

The monsignor turned and glared at him, the first time Nolan had seen anything but a positive emotion – friendliness, sympathy, or kindness – in his expression.

"It's preposterous. You say evidence. Usually the kind of evidence you have in a fire is just speculation because it's so burnt. Isn't that right? You shouldn't say evidence because it's not evidence if it doesn't prove something."

This took Nolan by surprise. "I, uh —"

"Evidence is something that proves something. At least

that's my understanding of the legal term."

"Sir, whatever you want to call it, there are, I guess you would say, strong indications, yes, strong indications that a fire was set to hide a robbery."

The monsignor blew his nose into his handkerchief.

"I just can't believe that a fire —"

Nolan waited for him to finish the sentence, but he did not.

Inquiries by Nolan at the Brooklyn Museum and at a Manhattan art gallery led to the information that the city's expert on the illegal trade in artworks was a man named Carl Jefferies.

Nolan located him at the Lenox Library at Fifth Avenue and 70th Street in Manhattan where he was curating an exhibition of watercolors about to open. Tall and sharply dressed, with a silk handkerchief in his breast pocket, Jefferies directed men in the hanging of the works, mostly those of Winslow Homer, while Nolan explained the circumstances of the theft of the Raphael.

"How big was the piece?" Jeffries asked.

"I've only seen a photograph, but two feet wide, three feet high, I would guess."

"If it was one of Raphael's bigger works, you'd have an easier time locating it. But it isn't. So let's start there. You've got one of his smaller pieces. If it was me who took this, I'd want to get it out of state to sell it."

"Out of state where?"

"Not Europe. The war is on. And not Boston or Chicago where they know art too well. Maybe a smaller city with some money. Maybe a St. Louis or a Denver or a city on the West Coast. There's a lot of money in

California right now and not a lot to buy out there in terms of important art. People want to brag about their money so they would love to own a Raphael to toss on their wall. So personally, yes, I'd send it to California."

"How would you send it? Roll up the canvas and ship it in a tube of some sort?"

Jefferies turned and raised an eyebrow. "Raphael didn't paint on canvas. He painted on wood."

"Wood?"

"A wood panel. Very thin. He liked to use chestnut, I believe."

Nolan had to think a moment. "Would this panel have burned any different than canvas?"

"Not at all. It was generally just a quarter inch thick, so once it got going, poof, it would go up in an instant."

Nolan showed him the evidence photographs of the charred frame. Seeing the unscorched back, Jeffries agreed the painting was removed before the fire.

"Do the photos tell you anything else?" Nolan asked.

"They tell me something very important."

"Yes?"

"Your thief is not a professional art thief. I knew that the minute you said he started a fire to hide what he did. In all my years, I've never encountered an art thief who tried to burn down the rest of the museum to hide his deed."

"And why's that?"

"Think about it. You have to have some knowledge of art, some appreciation, in order to know what to steal. So your nature would be averse to destroying art. My guess is your amateur would try to sell the piece at quite a discount to a greedy art dealer who would then ship it out of state. So I would go to the express companies and tell them to start looking for a flat crate of the size you indicated, marked fragile, on its way out west."

Across Fulton Street from the church was a grocery, Scibilia & Son, and at three o'clock in the afternoon it was filled with women lined up at the meat counter. Most, Nolan quickly learned, were parishioners of St. Mary's and for nearly fifteen uninterrupted minutes, he listened to praise for Monsignor Broydick and sympathy for the loss of his painting.

"If you go into any school in this part of Brooklyn, I would guess half the children were baptized by that man. The other half aren't Catholic," said one woman who was waiting for pork chops.

Told by Nolan the painting might have been stolen before the fire was set, she actually brightened. "It wasn't destroyed? My lord, it would be such a blessing if you could find his painting. To know the monsignor could retire and still have his beloved Raphael to keep him company in his last years, oh my lord, it would make many of us so happy."

There was an indoor flower mart near the grocery and Nolan came upon two women buying hothouse flowers who had seen the first fire engines arrive as they stood near the entrance of the grocery.

"We were chatting away out on the sidewalk," the more talkative of the two said.

"How long had you been chatting when the engines got there?"

The women looked at each other in a questioning manner. "Fifteen minutes?" the talkative woman guessed.

Two women buying flowers

"Did you see anything that looked out of the ordinary at or near the rectory in those fifteen minutes? Anything you can think of?"

Again, they looked at each other. The less talkative woman whispered to her friend, "The man with the ear."

"There was something," the talkative woman said. "We seen the monsignor go off somewhere, then we —"

"Go off with Miss Broydick?" Nolan asked.

"Yes, but I don't know that you should call her miss. I think she's a widow. I heard she married a railroad man when she was fifteen, and then he died two years later of something."

"So you saw the monsignor and his sister leave. What happened then?"

"Let's see," the talkative woman said. "A few minutes later, a man goes to the rectory door and knocks several times like it was important. When he gets no answer, he goes to one of the rectory windows and knocks a few times on the glass. I yells across that the monsignor wasn't there but I don't think he heard me 'cuz he kept knocking. Then he goes around the side of the rectory and I don't sees him again. And then five minutes later the fire starts up."

"Did either of you know the man?"

"I didn't," The less talkative woman said in a whisper. "But she did."

"I don't knows him, but I seen him before. Once I sat behind him at Mass and you know how in dull moments, you're looking all around, seeing what the other women are wearing? I notices he had a little chunk taken out of his earlobe on this side."

"The right side."

"Yes, his right earlobe. A little notch, like it got nicked by something. But you have to be right next to him to see it."

"Anything else you can think of?"

"One other thing about him. He's about thirty, your height maybe, but I seen his hair and thought, uh oh. A little gray around his ears. How quick that spreads. I ought to know. My husband had a little gray when I married him, but by forty, when he died, he was all gray."

Walking away, Nolan was pleased with himself. He had a suspect now. The man with the notched ear.

—◇—

His last stops in the afternoon were at the express freight offices in Brooklyn and southern Manhattan. He filled out reports describing the painting and its probable packaging and also left business cards with not only his telephone number but that of Stuyvesant at the insurance company.

On his way home, he began to look for the man with the nicked earlobe – on the elevated, walking the Brooklyn streets. First he looked for premature graying, and if he saw such a man, he would move closer. No luck.

From a news hawker near his tenement, Nolan picked up the evening edition of the *Brooklyn Daily Eagle* and stood on the sidewalk as a light snow fell, reading the account of the elevator accident and the unsuccessful attempt to save the boy earlier that afternoon.

"His body came out of the elevator but his soul did not," the monsignor was quoted as saying.

He threw the newspaper in a public garbage can before going in his building. He knew the story would upset Sheenagh for the rest of the evening if she read it.

She was in the kitchen and he could smell the soup. Even before he asked, she handed him a spoon for a sample.

"I took a message while you were out," she said. "It's by the instrument."

"The telephone?"

"Yes. If you can't read it, it's because I couldn't understand a word he said. He was German, I think. He called a few minutes ago."

Had the German understood her? In his two years in the city, his Irish accent had softened, drifting closer to the American voice, but Sheenagh had lost none of hers – and likely never would, he realized, out of a stubborn Irish pride that would not allow it.

In the living room by the telephone, Nolan found the message scribbled on grocer's paper that had apparently wrapped chicken at some point, judging by the smell. He went to the kitchen door. "Do you mean he spoke in German or that he had a German accent?"

"He was trying to speak English but it sounded German to me."

"What's this mean? ... 'Depending on the form.'"

"That's what it sounded like to me. He kept saying it. I hoped you'd know what it meant."

"Did he give his name?"

"I couldn't understand it. It's that last bit. Frank something. Frank Press maybe."

"Did he leave a telephone number?"

"No. He said he'd call back."

"Depending on the form. Could that have been ... the painting on the form?"

"What would that sound like if a German said it?"

Nolan smiled. If a German said it and an Irish girl heard it – indeed, what would that sound like?

A police sergeant at the Washington Street station house recalled a man who lived up near the Brooklyn Navy Yard who fit the description – premature gray hair and a mangled ear. "George Waters or Watson or something like that. I arrested him once for burglary," he told Nolan. "He lived on one of those streets what goes right by the yard."

That afternoon, with the late fall sun shining, Nolan took a trolley to the Navy Yard, which was busy with work on new battleships in case America entered the war.

He planned to go door to door to ask about such a man. Beginning on a street of three-story, brick tenements that dead-ended at the East River, he glanced up at the rooftop and saw a boy, perhaps fifteen, jumping from building to building, then looking over the high Navy Yard fence as if searching for a good place to jump in.

Nolan yelled up at him. "Hey, get off there!"

The boy reached into his back pocket and produced a revolver. As soon as Nolan saw the black barrel, he dropped behind a parked automobile. A shot rang out. To his left, about thirty yards away, Nolan saw a spray of dust kick up off the cobblestone street. He took out his own revolver and rose.

Now a police officer, a heavy man, appeared atop the roof of the last tenement that was right up against the river. The boy, about thirty yards away, pointed his revolver toward the policeman, who, in trying to steady himself, lost his footing and toppled backwards into the river, landing with a splash.

Nolan fired at the boy, not intending to hit him, just to warn him off, and the boy ran but was almost immediately grabbed by two officers, guns drawn, who had climbed onto the roofs from the Navy Yard side.

Nolan rushed to the river. The shore was a mixture of thin ice and flowing water and the officer was face down in the water about twenty feet from the shore, floating slowly toward New York Bay. Nolan cursed under his breath and waded in, shocked by how cold the water was. Losing a shoe in the muddy bottom, he made a grab at the officer's foot as it went by, quickly turned the man over to get his face out of the water. With the man coughing and spitting, Nolan began to pull his heavy body toward the riverbank, cursing at the frigidness of the water and losing his other shoe.

⋘⟐⋙

One of the officers was giving Nolan a ride home in his police motor. Shoeless, soaking wet, and wrapped in a wool blanket, Nolan sat in the back seat.

"Could you do me a favor?" Nolan asked. "Could you not give the newspapers my name? If my wife reads about this, she'll be angry I was in a gun battle."

"What're you going to tell her?"

"That a child fell in the river and I pulled him out."

"Who was this man you were looking for in the first place? I know that neighborhood."

"George Waters or Watson maybe. About my age, some gray hair, a bad ear."

"George Waterston. I know him well. He's been living upstate in Ossining for the past two years."

"Where the state prison is?"

"In fact, that's his address. You can write him there for at least the next ten years."

"Oh."

"And he ain't got a bad ear. He's got no ear. It got shot off. Doesn't sound like this is your man."

—◆—

In the morning, he was again at the offices of Federated Insurance.

"I'm here to see Mr. Stuyvesant."

"Do you have an appointment?" It was the same receptionist as in his first visit.

"No, but —"

"You can't see him without an appointment."

"He was the one who called me."

"You still need an appointment. Did he give you one?"

Nolan gritted his teeth. "He called me this morning and said it was important to come in, so I advise you to go get the man."

Now Nolan saw Stuyvesant walking nearby and

advanced past her desk. "Never mind."

The receptionist began to protest, but Stuyvesant, seeing him, called out his name as he approached. Stuyvesant offered his hand, which Nolan shook with some suspicion. Friendliness was not a trait of character he remembered in him.

Stuyvesant picked up papers off his desk, and they moved to the same oak-paneled conference room as before. He seemed to enjoy installing himself in the chair at the head of the table. A massive green globe of the world was on a pedestal just behind him.

"The reason I called is the company wants to, well, to make a generous show of, uh, a show of goodwill in terms of the St. Mary's fire. We want to make a gesture to the parish and settle the claim of the pastor. Is that what you call him? A pastor? I'm not Catholic."

The assumption was that Nolan was Irish so he was Catholic. While it was true, he resented it. "Pastor is good enough. He's a monsignor."

"Whatever the man is, we want to settle. So in the matter of the painting – I know that's the most expensive thing on the list – we'd like to settle for that first to show our heart is in the right place. This is the paper we'd like you to get the pastor ..." Stuyvesant glanced at the document as he prepared to slide it across the table "... Broydick. Robert A. Broydick. We want you to have him sign it, and here, this is a check for the full amount it was insured, $28,000, made out to him."

Nolan studied both the form and the check.

"We want to be a friend to the Brooklyn community," Stuyvesant said, rising from the table. "And we feel this would show that we're making a gesture of goodwill, uh, toward the community ... One thing. My experience is that if you wave the check in front of him, let him see it, then he'll sign as fast as you can get a pen in his hand."

Nolan looked up at Stuyvesant, who had turned away to twirl the globe a few spins. Goodwill indeed. Something was going on.

—◈—

In its Wednesday edition, the *Brooklyn Daily Eagle* reported the "heroic rescue" of a police officer at the Navy Yard the day before and the role in it of private detective John Nolan.

Nolan was unaware of this, but Sheenagh learned of it at the market while he was at the insurance company. When he got home, she was waiting for him in the front room and was furious.

"I have to hear about it from the green grocer, not my own husband!"

"I worried you would be mad."

"Well, you got your wish. I am mad."

"It sounds more dangerous that it was. His shot missed me by quite a distance."

"What shot? This man shot at you?"

"It didn't say that in the story?"

"No, it didn't, John!"

Nolan told her all of it, emphasizing his distance from the man on the roof when he fired and his precautions whenever in danger.

"You say you shot at him. Did you hit him?"

"No."

"Why not?"

"I wasn't trying to hit him, just warn him off."

"If you had been trying to hit him, could you of?

Could you defend yourself, if you had to?"

"Could I hit him? Of course I could. I'm a good shot."

"Have you been shot at before?"

"I'm not going to tell you, but I'm still here, aren't I?"

She studied him and slowly shook her head. "Men." Then she walked out of the room.

The monsignor's sister answered the rectory door, not smiling at all as she let him in. In fact, he realized he had never seen her smile. ("A belligerent woman," he once overhead a parishioner say. "You go to see the monsignor and she orders you around like she thinks she's the pope.")

She said the monsignor was down the hall in the sitting room writing a eulogy. The door was open but Nolan knocked anyway. The monsignor, seated in a large plush chair by the fireplace, looked up.

"Father. Can we talk a moment?"

"I need to take a breather, so, yes, please have a seat."

"Sir, I've been to the insurance company and they've made an interesting offer. They want to settle your claim for the painting. It would just be for your painting at this point and not the books."

The monsignor frowned and looked away, which surprised Nolan.

"Sir, it's for the full insured amount, $28,000. They've even given me the check."

The monsignor rose, picked up the poker, and nudged the glowing logs to raise a flame. Many framed family photographs were atop the mantle. He picked up one then another and distractedly studyied them. "Unfortunately, there's a problem. I feel reluctant to take the money, to be honest, and it relates to the problem."

Nolan waited.

"The Raphael was purchased by my great-great-grandfather who was a solicitor in Boston ... Boston, England, not Massachusetts."

"Yes, sir."

"Well, years went by, the family came to America, and when my mother died, I inherited it. Wondering how much to insure it for, I took it to an art dealer here in the city, an expert, and got his opinion. And that's the problem."

The monsignor, still gazing at the fire, was silent.

"Sir?"

"He thought it might be a fake, a good fake, but a fake. He said you had poor artists who would go to the museums of Europe and copy the works of a master, then go home and take elements of the man's various paintings and create a new work by him. Then, they would go abroad to a place where men had money but were not well versed in art and try to sell it as an original. This dealer – that's what he suspected was going on. He said the Madonna's head looked to be very similar to the Madonna's head in another Raphael he knew intimately, and the masters didn't repeat themselves."

"If it was a good fake, then what's it worth?"

"I ... I can't say. Perhaps a few hundred dollars."

"But you had it insured for $28,000."

The monsignor turned. "What would you have done? I was a younger man and, at the time, I thought that was appropriate, given that the dealer wasn't sure if it was real or not. If it was real, it was worth ten times the $28,000. Ten times at least. So I chose that figure. A compromise that I thought was fair." He turned back to the window. "It was the best I could do at the time."

"Sir, it strikes me that it's still fair. The issue of it being real or a fraud isn't settled. You should take the money."

The monsignor sighed. "My conscience won't let me now. I'm older and ... well, my conscience will not permit it."

⸪

Seeing him approach the front desk, the receptionist conspicuously turned back to the files she was organizing and did not look up again. He took this to mean she was not going to interrogate him this time. As he passed, he saw Stuyvesant come out of an office down the hallway and glance in his direction.

"I'm glad you're here," Stuyvesant said. He briefly returned to the office and came out with a sheet in his hands. "I've got the list of books the pastor is claiming and how much he says they're worth and, no, this will not do at all."

He handed the sheet to Nolan. There were nine titles along with their insured amounts.

"Alice's Adventures in Wonderland"
– Carroll, 1866, $160
"The Strange Gentleman" –
Dickens, 1837, $325
"Poems" – Keats, 1817, $500

The other titles were by authors Nolan did not recognize.

"This is what I want you do to," Stuyvesant said. "Go to three book dealers in the city, see if they have any of these titles or can get them, and find out what the cost would be. Then we'll offer to pay Broydick fifty percent of whatever the lowest price is for each."

"Aren't you supposed to pay the replacement cost?"

"If you went to a hundred dealers my guess is at least one would have one of them for fifty percent less. So that's the replacement price."

"Who would go to one hundred bookshops to replace just one book?"

"Just do what I say."

Nolan frowned, folded the list, and put it in his inside pocket. At the same time, he took out the unsigned form and the check.

"Here's the bank check back. He wouldn't take it."

"What do you mean he wouldn't take it? Why for God's sake?"

"He's a principled man, as you would expect a monsignor to be. He feels ..." On a sudden instinct, Nolan decided to lie. "He feels he did nothing to earn the money as it was a distant relative what purchased the painting and not him."

"He owned the damn thing, though. He inherited it."

"That's how he feels. He did buy the first editions, though. And he wants to be paid for those, paid a fair price. Those were his words. A fair price."

Stuyvesant grimaced. "No," he said. "You go to him and make this argument. You say, Mr. Broydick —"

"Monsignor."

"You say, Monsignor Broydick, kind sir, this check for $28,000 would be a great benefit to the orphans and widows of this city. The New York Federated Insurance Company is intent on making a gesture of goodwill to you and to your, uh, to your Catholic followers. So I ask you. How can a man not take money that can be donated to orphans and widows and then say this is to soothe his conscience? Can such a man even claim to have a conscience?" Stuyvesant looked pleased with himself. "Yes. You say that to him. He'll sign, if I'm any judge."

—◆—

The monsignor heard the argument, delivered without much conviction by Nolan, then completely surprised him by signing the form. "I ask one thing. Don't give me the check. Take it to the bank and donate it to Catholic Relief Fund for the Children's Court."

Nolan left, believing that it took a mind he could not comprehend to become a priest in the first place, to give up the pleasures of marriage, so why try to comprehend what a priest thinks about anything?

—◆—

The next morning, he took the subway into Manhattan and stopped by the Federated Insurance office to drop off the signed form at the receptionist's desk. Then he went directly to the New York Public Library. He had borrowed the photograph of the Raphael from the insurance company and wanted to settle a question for himself.

He located three books with color plates of Renaissance art, including one with a chapter devoted to Raphael. He went from book to book, comparing the paintings to the photograph.

He shook his head. It was astonishing how little effort the copyist made to hide what he had done. The face of the Madonna was identical to that in "Madonna with Child and Saints." The upper half of the baby Jesus matched that in "Solly Madonna," and the lower half and much of the rest of the painting matched "Madonna

The insurance photograph of the Raphael

and Child with the Book." Such artless fakery, he thought.

In his own mind, Nolan easily justified that he was not going to tell Stuyvesant about this. The form was signed by the monsignor before Nolan became convinced the painting was likely a fake. So legally the money was at that point the monsignor's. Also, the insurance company wanted to make a gesture of goodwill to the Brooklyn parish, and that is what they were doing. The money went to needy children. In any case, to hell with Stuyvesant as he was intent on cheating the monsignor on his first editions anyway.

At Canal Street, he took the subway back to Brooklyn. As the car pulled in to the DeKalb Avenue station, he spotted Catherine Broydick on the platform, waiting to get on for the trip farther south toward Coney Island. She was holding what looked to be a half dozen rolls of wallpaper under one arm.

He got off the car and immediately ducked behind a large stanchion, out of sight, weighing whether he wanted to be seen by her and have to speak to her. After all, she was an unpleasant woman, the opposite of her brother. However, she quickly stepped into the car, relieving him of the decision.

The Mass at St. Mary of the Assumption Sunday morning was crowded, and Sheenagh was disappointed they could only find seats in the second to the last row of pews.

During the service, each time they rose to sing, Nolan would survey the heads around him, looking for a man about his age with gray at the temples. He saw no one who raised suspicion.

It turned out to be a lengthy Mass, with a sermon by the monsignor about frugality that went on forever. However, it was the moment they would leave that Nolan was anticipating.

Finally, the blessing was given and the dismissal spoken. ("You may go in peace.") Then the monsignor strode down the center aisle as "For All the Saints" played. The pews emptied as the organ filled the church.

He and Sheenagh took their place near the front of the line as the monsignor greeted each person on the steps outside the large oaken doors, offering a word or two and clasping their hand or shoulder. Finally, Sheenagh reached him.

"Why you must be Sheenagh, John's beautiful wife," he said, taking both her hands in his.

Sheenagh's face flushed and her eyes moistened. "Oh, Monsignor, bless you. It was a wonderful, wonderful

Mass and we'll be back every week. Bless you, Father. Bless you."

"And Sheenagh, please come in and see me and we'll set a date for the baptism. Will you do that?"

"Oh, yes, Father, bless you so much. I certainly will."

Overcome, she proceeded down the steps, dabbing her eyes with her handkerchief.

As Nolan shook his hand, the monsignor winked.

That evening, in his living room, putting paperwork and other material related to the case into his file drawer, Nolan studied the extra evidence photographs that had not been given to the insurance company since nothing in them was burned. There were several of the sitting room in which he had met with the monsignor, including close-up views of the bookcase to the side of the fireplace, all taken the morning after the fire.

Nolan tried to find differences in the photographs compared to his recent memory of the room. For one thing, in the photographs, the monsignor's heavy plush chair was not by the fireplace. It was not even in the room. What did that mean? For another, the framed family photographs were missing from atop the mantle.

He looked closer at the evidence photos. He realized he could read the titles on the bookshelves. He drew out the list of first editions in the claim from his file drawer. What if, in comparing them, he saw a title on the list and on the bookshelf? People did that sort of thing, claimed ruined items in a fire – that were never ruined – for the insurance money. He shook his head at his own lack of faith. After all, this was the monsignor. And what if he found a title on the list and on the shelf. What would he do then? Turn the man in? He realized he did not want to know and filed away the photos.

Monday afternoon, he worked at his desk while Sheenagh went to the market. The ringing bell of the telephone, which sat inches away on his desk, startled him.

"Hello. Nolan Detective Bureau."

Something was said by the man on the other end, but the German accent was so heavy and the words came so fast he could not understand any of it.

"Sir, can you repeat that and speak slower please?"

What Nolan eventually understood is that the man was an agent for a freight express company in the city (thus Sheenagh's 'Frank Press,' he realized) and was calling to get money he was owed.

"De insurance man – he promised I vud get a reward if I give him da painting."

"Federated Insurance?"

"Ya. Dis card you gave me. I called his number you has on it. He comes and he gets da painting and said he give me a check, but he left and didn't give me no check. So you should pay me. I vant de reward."

"You're talking about the Raphael painting?"

"Ya. Da stolen painting I found. He says I get a reward for finding it. I vant the money."

"Sir, I'll go to the insurance company and ask them to pay you what they promised. What's your name and address please?"

Nolan wrote the information down, including the payment promised, fifty dollars.

"And could you tell me when the Federated man came

by to get the painting? Was it today?"

"Dis vas last week."

"Last week? You're sure?"

"Ya."

"What was the date he came last week?"

The man could be heard shuffling papers about. "Dis says ... November second."

Nolan looked at his appointment calendar. Federated had pushed him to get the monsignor to sign the papers the next day, November third.

"I found it just as it vas about to be shipped out," the freight man said. "Just like you describe it. It say 'fragile painting' right on da package like you said. Dis man, da insurance man, he bring a photograph if it vit him. Ve look at dem both. Day vas de same painting. So I gives it to him and signs some papers. But he promise me a reward and he don't give me no check."

"I'll go talk to him."

The receptionist glanced up, saw him, and then returned her eyes to whatever she was doing. Nolan found Stuyvesant in one of the large offices down the hallway. He was sitting at a massive mahogany desk with an aquarium behind him.

He looked up. "It's good you're here. Let's use the conference room."

They went down the hall and once inside, Stuyvesant closed the door and handed Nolan a sheet of paper. "We didn't like the numbers you gave us on the first editions, so we're going lower."

Nolan did not take the sheet. "You recovered the Raphael."

Stuyvesant regarded him suspiciously. "Yes, we did."

"But you recovered it before the monsignor signed the claim form?"

"I don't recall the exact dates."

"Well, I know the exact dates. You misrepresented the facts to me. You sent me out to get him to sign without telling me you had his painting."

"John, sit down."

"No."

Stuyvesant sat anyway, then saw the disadvantage this gave him in the conversation and awkwardly stood again. "Look, we're in a business here and we do what we need to do sometimes. Yes, we may have gotten the painting before the monsignor signed, but we paid him the full estimate he gave us for its worth. So in my mind we're even."

"You deliberately —"

"We did what we had to do."

Nolan shook his head in mild disgust, then he put the paper with the information about the shipping agent's reward on the conference table and shoved it across to Stuyvesant. "By the way, this man expects the reward you promised. He earned it, I would say."

As Stuyvesant read the page, Nolan studied him. "So you decided this Raphael, this original Raphael, is worth so much more than the estimate that you were willing to pay off the claim so you could keep the painting."

Stuyvesant only smiled.

"Did you have the painting valued?" Nolan asked.

"Our president did, yes. He has a brother who's a collector. He's been to auctions in Italy where Raphaels sold for hundreds of thousands of dollars, and he looked at our Raphael. So yes, we know the value."

"The brother of the company's president."

"He's a collector, yes."

"And no one else looked at it?"

"His brother knows quite a bit about art, our president said."

Nolan held back a laugh. "What about the person who shipped the painting? They were either the thief or they bought it from the thief. Do you want me to question this person?"

"We had one of our people try to track him down. He gave the shipping man an alias. I'm guessing he bought the Raphael from the thief. But whoever it was, you won't find him."

"Won't he come forward when his painting doesn't arrive wherever it was going? Won't he want it back?"

"If he does, we'll deal with him. It's none of your concern. But I'm guessing he'll never come forward or else be charged with receiving stolen artwork or actually stealing it in the first place."

"What about the place it was being shipped?"

"A post office box in Seattle. That name – the man who rented the box – was also an alias. My guess is they're both part of an art theft ring."

Nolan considered the situation. "So this is done then, this case, other than the first editions."

"Your part of it is done, yes. We own the painting, the monsignor has his check. So yes. It's done. If it was arson, it was arson, but we're satisfied."

Nolan buttoned his overcoat, preparing to leave. "And now you own a very valuable Raphael."

Again, Stuyvesant only smiled.

Rioting broke out in Williamsburg, a poor district of Brooklyn, as women attacked peddlers and set fire to their pushcarts over rising food prices. Onions had jumped five cents a pound overnight as had the cost of potatoes. Thousands of women took to the streets and the police reserves were called out to restore order.

Mr. Shapiro, their upstairs neighbor, came to Nolan around lunch saying his wife had gone to Roebling Street in Williamsburg to see her cousin that morning and had not returned. Could he go look for her?

"I know you have a gun and you're a fit man. I have neither – a gun or health."

Nolan took a trolley to the outskirts of the district then walked. On Grand Street, there was a mob of nearly a hundred women, some with torches made of rolled newspapers, facing a line of uniformed reserves, the two groups shouting at each other. And on South Third Street, he had to walk around a pushcart on its side and in flames, roasted carrots spilling onto the sidewalk. Other pushcarts around it were just smoking, charred debris.

On Roebling Street, though, the rioting had been brought under control by the reserves. The street was largely cleared. He spotted Mrs. Shapiro standing with other women on the front stoop of her cousin's tenement.

"Your husband sent me. He was worried."

"I didn't want to make the walk back with everything going on, but aren't you good for coming to fetch me. You tell Mr. Shapiro I'm going to stay until the last policeman is gone, though. They're arresting women just for being a woman walking along the street right now."

Nolan gave her a nickel and told her there was a trolley stop a block south if she wanted to avoid the walk home.

With the skies turning dark, he decided to take the trolley himself. He boarded an open-sided car at Union Avenue, walked up the aisle, and took an empty seat. Idly looking around, his eyes fell on a man sitting directly behind the motorman. He was about Nolan's age with gray around his ears. However, he could not see the man's right earlobe from where he sat, so he moved to a seat across the aisle, waited a moment so as not to be conspicuous, then glanced over at the man's ear.

Indeed, there was a small notch, a missing chunk of flesh, on the bottom of the lobe. Seeing it, Nolan's pulse jumped.

As the trolley bumped along, he tried to formulate a plan. First, he tried to assess the man's employment. His hands were clean, but his suit, while clean, was badly rumpled. He was not a laborer but he was not a lawyer either. Second, he tried to gauge the man's size. He seemed no bigger than Nolan and was likely less experienced in a fight. That was good. However, Nolan reminded himself this man was not guilty of anything yet. He had only been seen near a building that caught fire.

The man got off at DeKalb to pick up another trolley, so Nolan did as well, pushing into the crowd of people also waiting at the sidewalk stop. A light sleet had begun to fall and Nolan closed the top button on his overcoat and pulled his derby down tight. Soon a westbound trolley arrived and the man took a seat near the front again, so Nolan took one as far to the rear as possible.

When the man rose to get off at Putnam Avenue,

Nolan rose. When the man walked west on the sidewalk, Nolan walked west, keeping thirty paces behind. That the man never glanced back told Nolan he suspected nothing. The sleet continued.

At a tenement on Putnam, the man walked up the steps to the door.

"Excuse me. Aren't you a parishioner of St. Mary's?" Nolan asked.

The man turned but did not answer immediately. "...Yes."

"So am I." He stepped forward and extended his hand. "My name is John Nolan."

With some uncertainty, the man shook Nolan's hand.

"Let me ask you." Nolan said. "I don't know if you heard, but there was a fire in the rectory."

"I heard."

"Would you mind if I talk to you a minute?"

"Look, I have someone waiting for me inside. Maybe we'll talk at church sometime, if you're raising funds for it."

"It's about how the fire started." Nolan said, which stopped the man. Nolan took out his private detective's badge, which, when flashed quickly, could be mistaken for a police badge. "I'm a detective."

Fear came into the man's expression.

With the sleet growing heavier, Nolan suggested they go into the front hallway. The man complied, leading him in. Nolan made sure to unbutton his overcoat to have his revolver handy.

"Let's use my apartment upstairs," the man said and Nolan nodded, moving his revolver to his coat pocket as they began the climb.

The stairwell was lit by one flickering electric light, and the rickety stair railing was missing balusters. At the top of the first floor landing, the man unlocked an apartment door. His hand on his revolver, Nolan pushed closer to him in case he might decide to slam it in Nolan's face and lock it quickly.

Inside, the front room was well furnished. There was the hand of a woman at work, Nolan thought – flowers in vases, bright curtains, lace antimacassars on the sofa arms.

The man turned. "What do you want to talk to me about?"

A girl, perhaps fifteen of sixteen, with black braided hair came to the kitchen door. Thin as a rod, she was shoeless and dressed in a simple house dress.

"You were seen by several women just before the fire broke out, knocking on the rectory door and on a window, like there was some urgency to getting in."

The man stared at Nolan. "So what?"

"Why were you there?"

"All I did was knock on the rectory door. How many times a day does someone knock on the rectory door? A dozen? My guess is you've knocked on that door yourself. What does that prove?"

"I wasn't the one seen just before a fire started."

"How does knocking on a door start a fire?"

"You were also seen going around back of the rectory when no one answered."

"Who said this? Those women said this?"

"They did."

"Well, you tell them to mind their own business."

"Again, why were you there?"

The man looked over at the girl in the kitchen door. "It's personal why I was there."

"I think you better tell me." Nolan said.

Again, the man looked over at the girl but she turned her eyes to the floor.

"I wanted the monsignor to marry us," he said. "I needed him to marry us quick. Zaira and I, we had an urgent need at the time to be married quick."

Nolan could guess why. However, he saw no evidence of a pregnancy in the girl.

"What did the monsignor say?"

"He wasn't there that day and I didn't go back. I guess the need disappeared."

Nolan turned to the girl. "Is this true?"

She frowned then went back into the kitchen.

"Zaira, tell the man. Is there a need anymore to get married?"

Once again, she came to the door. "A need? If you love someone, there's a need ... if you love someone."

All three were silent.

"Did you lose a baby?" Nolan finally asked her.

"I didn't lose it. A woman took it out of me with an instrument." With that, she went back into the kitchen and the man, seeming to believe Nolan had heard all he needed to hear, lit a cigarette and sat on the sofa, watching him.

"Something else, detective?"

Nolan thought a moment then turned to the door. "I guess not. Sorry I bothered you."

—◈—

Nolan dropped off his bill and final report at Federated Insurance, frustrated that he had not solved the case but happy to take the insurance company's money. Returning to Brooklyn by subway, he again saw Catherine Broydick on the platform as the car pulled into the DeKalb Avenue station. This time, he could not avoid her.

"Miss Broydick. Nice to see you. Where are you off to?"

"Nowhere. I'm meeting someone," she said gruffly. She had a pile of fabric samples under her arm.

"Giving them those?"

She gazed at him, as if not understanding.

"The material. Are you giving those pieces to someone?"

Her expression turned sour. "I don't expect that's your business."

Nolan did not know how to react, so he tipped his derby. "I guess it isn't. Have a good day, Miss Broydick."

He walked toward the platform exit, thinking. Of course, she was going somewhere. You do not pay your fare then go down on the platform just to meet someone. You meet them beyond the gate.

As he approached the exit, he glanced back. She was turned away, waiting for the crowds to empty out of the car. Nolan ducked behind a stanchion, removing his derby so he could peer around its edge to see her undetected. She looked in his direction, seemed to think he had gone through the gate, so she made a movement to get on the last car. Nolan darted onto the first.

The Fourth Avenue subway had a route that took it down the coast of Brooklyn, past views of Manhattan, New York Harbor, and the Statue of Liberty. New residential communities had sprung up all along the line.

At each stop – Atlantic Avenue, Union Street, Prospect Avenue – he went to the door as it opened, glanced back to see if she had exited, then moved back into the car.

At the 59th Street station, she did disembark and begin walking down the steps. He followed her up Fourth Avenue, staying behind at a good distance. A small, waddling woman was not about to lose him.

The neighborhood into which she walked – Sunset Park – was one of neat, new, limestone and brownstone row houses. The latest Dodges, Fords, and Hudsons were parked on the street.

She turned at 57th and then walked through the iron gate of a two-story, brick and limestone row house. Masons were atop a scaffold working on the decorative cornice along the roof. Painters were on the ground touching up the window trim.

On scrap paper in his pocket, Nolan wrote down the address.

"How would I find who holds the new deed to this property?"

He turned his paper toward the registry clerk.

"Go upstairs, second door on the right. That fellow will have the most recent book if it just sold. Tell him it'll be in the current book, the number six register."

Upstairs, the clerk was out and the office empty. However, Nolan could see the thick register books in a haphazard pile atop the closest desk. He went over and opened the number six book.

535 57th Street – $9,340 – Miss
Catherine Broydick, buyer – V.R.

Rheingold and Co., seller – No mortgage held – Oct. 29, 1915

"Excuse me. Did anyone say you could go through that book?" The clerk had returned.

"No one said I couldn't and there was no one on duty. Can I ask you what this means? No mortgage?"

The clerk sighed, seemed to realize Nolan was not going to feel any guilt, and came over to peer at the entry.

"No mortgage means paid in cash."

Awake after midnight, as Nolan ran things through his mind, it was impossible for suspicions not to take hold. As he was about to fall asleep, something else occurred to him. It was what he had seen in a photograph two days earlier.

He quietly slipped out of bed so as to not wake Sheenagh, then went to the living room where he kept his

The insurance photograph of the rectory sitting room

case files. He lit a kerosene lamp and looked again at the photographs taken the morning after the fire, the left-overs not given to Federated Insurance.

In his meetings in the rectory sitting room with the monsignor, there had been framed family photographs on the fireplace mantle to the left of a clock. Yet, those photographs were missing in the evidence photos that showed the fireplace. What if the photos had been on the mantle for years? What if someone who thought the rectory was about to be destroyed had taken them away just prior to the fire's start? What if that same person, seeing the rectory had survived largely intact, returned them to the mantle the next day – after the evidence photos were taken?

Suspicions could only stay mere suspicions for so long.

———◇———

"Would you mind if I closed the door? This is private," Nolan said.

"Go ahead," the monsignor answered.

Nolan did and then sat in a chair near the sitting room fireplace, pulling it a bit closer to the monsignor's chair. The monsignor seemed to sense the importance and pushed his cup of tea away.

"First, I'm very sorry about, well, about what I'm going to tell you. I haven't told this to anyone at the insurance company and I don't plan to until you've had your chance to think about it."

"My goodness. The suspense is probably worse than whatever your news is, so just go ahead."

Nolan told the monsignor about twice running into his sister at the DeKalb Avenue station and then following her the second time when she lied about why she was there. He described the row house she went into in Sunset

Park and the discovery of the deed in her name. Then he showed the monsignor the photographs of the very sitting room they were in, with the family photographs not on the mantle the morning after the fire.

"She told me once that she lost her inheritance in the panic. So where did she get the money for the row house? And these missing photographs on the mantle. My belief is they were taken out of here by someone who valued those memories and believed the rectory was about to be lost ... Sir, do you see where this is leading?"

The monsignor stared at him.

"Sir, do you see?"

"No. No, I don't," he said angrily. "This is just guesswork. It's ... It's insulting."

"Sir, where did your sister get the money to buy that residence?"

The monsignor stood and walked to the rectory window.

"Sir?"

"This is ... maybe it isn't preposterous on its face, but ..." He turned. "But my sister would never, never do something like you're suggesting. She's been at my side for the twenty-five years I've been in this parish. I know her better than I, well, almost as well as I know myself."

"The evidence —"

"It may say what it seems to say, but I'm telling you ..." He turned again to the window, shaking his head. "My sister *did not* do this."

"Do you know for a fact? Do you have some evidence that explains these things?"

The monsignor, continuing to stare out the window, said nothing.

"Sir?"

"What happens now?" the monsignor asked.

"If you can't come up with substantial reasons why the evidence is pointing in the wrong direction, I have to go to the fire inspector and I suppose I have to go to the insurance company."

"Can you give me some time?"

"To talk to your sister? Yes, I can."

"Can you give me a week?"

"A week is a little long, but, yes, I can give you a week."

The monsignor was still gazing out the window as Nolan left.

As it had been every Sunday recently, the Mass at St. Mary's was crowded. Sheenagh made him leave their apartment a half hour early, and still, they could not find seats in the front half of the church.

Nolan had not told Sheenagh of his mounting suspicions about the monsignor's sister. Sheenagh had been to tea at the rectory, met the sister, and was one of the few who liked her. ("I thought her an extremely lovely person.") So there would be no domestic peace in their home if she knew the theory he was pursuing.

During the Mass, Nolan watched the monsignor closely, looking for signs of his distress. Here was a man who was weighing a decision that could ruin his sister's life and perhaps his own. Might he lose the parish? The Catholic Church could be severe in its punishments.

During the homily, Nolan was sure the monsignor might fall apart. After a Scripture reading about personal charity, he began to preach frantically about "the terrible squalor much of the world experiences," and the "individual's responsibility to act to relieve it." The monsignor seemed almost moved to tears by his apparent compassion. His weekly homilies, until then, had been measured and unemotional, kindly bits of advice.

Afterward, as they met the monsignor at the door, he clasped Sheenagh's hand warmly.

"Dear, we'll have to begin to think about a date for the baptism," he told her. "It will get done."

"Oh, Father, I so look forward to it."

When Nolan stepped up, the monsignor took his hand and smiled, but almost immediately reached for the next hand in line.

As Nolan walked down the stairs, though, he heard the monsignor call after him.

"John, I didn't say it, but thank you for coming."

Nolan turned and waved.

The knocking at their front door Monday morning was insistent. Nolan, in only his trousers, was eating breakfast in the kitchen. Sheenagh, washed and dressed, went to answer it. Nolan heard a woman's voice crying as much as talking. He also heard the monsignor's name.

He pulled on his shirt and rushed to the living room. However, the woman had gone and Sheenagh was in tears, collapsed onto the sofa.

"What happened? Sheenagh, please dear. What's happened?"

She curled up into herself and began to wail and roll from side to side.

"Sheenagh, please. What?"

"The monsignor, oh, my dear God, the monsignor has been killed, oh, my dear, dear God, oh God!"

At the Poplar Street police station, crowded with St. Mary's parishioners wanting news, he learned what had happened.

At just before seven o'clock that morning, the monsignor had been going on foot to visit a family on Henry Street concerning the failing health of their invalid daughter, a sergeant told him.

"The witness we talked to said the monsignor, bless him, he took a step off the curb on Flatbush Avenue without properly looking, as if his mind was somewhere else, and he walked right into the path of a motor truck. He was thrown half a block and killed in an instant. What a shame. My own wife – he baptized her and he married us. What a terrible tragedy."

Numbed, Nolan moved to a corner of the room. Around him women cried and policemen tried to soothe them and clear the room. However, more people came through the door than went out and Nolan found himself pressed against the wall, unable to move.

He shut his eyes. The monsignor had crossed Flatbush thousands of times. Was he so distracted by what Nolan told him about his sister, so consumed by the burden of his thoughts, that he failed to take the simple precaution to look up? Had what Nolan put in his mind been too heavy a load for such an elderly man?

Fighting his own emotions, Nolan pushed his way through the throng toward the door. He was not convinced he was to blame, but he was also not convinced he was not. And for him, that was as good as being pronounced guilty by a court. He would never be able to feel completely innocent of the man's death. He knew that for a fact.

---⟨◈⟩---

The funeral two days later was going to be one of the largest Brooklyn had ever experienced. More than 300 police reserves were set to be called out. However, Nolan told Sheenagh that morning that he was ill and would be unable to attend. (In fact, he worried the monsignor had told the sister of his suspicions and that she would confront him with mourners all around.)

Instead of Sheenagh seeing this for the excuse it was, though, she seemed to forgive him, apparently believing it was evidence of his deep feelings for the monsignor. Indeed, he had been physically sickened by his death.

However, after Sheenagh left, he almost did grow sick thinking about what he had to do next – take his suspicions about the monsignor's sister to the police and fire department investigators.

---⟨◈⟩---

The *Brooklyn Daily Eagle* issued a special afternoon edition with the story of the funeral taking up nearly the entire front page. Nolan was on the street to buy it even before Sheenagh returned home.

FUNERAL FOR BELOVED PRIEST

Monsignor Broydick laid to rest

Mourners silent and sad

Archbishop accompanies body

A large gold crucifix gracing the lid of his coffin, the body of Monsignor Robert Ambrose Broydick was borne to Holy Cross Cemetery in a horse-drawn trolley car this morning.

The funeral car containing the black coffin was followed by fifteen trolley cars filled with mourners and then by a crowd of more than a thousand, many of them brought to tears by the spectacle and the tragedy.

During his years of ministration among the poor, Father Broydick always preached against expensive funerals and he died by the principles with which he lived.

Father Broydick was killed Monday when he was struck by a motor truck while crossing Flatbush Avenue.

The crowds for the funeral Mass at St. Mary of the Assumption at ten o'clock could not be contained in the Fulton Street church. Police reserves had to keep order.

Monsignor Broydick, 69, was a close friend of Cardinal Farley and was elevated to monsignor at the same time as the cardinal received

the "red hat."

"He was called the saint of Brooklyn," the cardinal said. "And it was for a good reason. His duty to God and his parish never flagged."

After a sleepless night, created as much by Sheenagh's frequent trips to the living room to cry as by his own despair over what he might have caused, Nolan rose early. He kept to himself at his small desk in the living room while Sheenagh sewed in the bedroom.

Hearing the clatter of the postman in the front hall, Nolan waited for him to leave then went out and retrieved the small number of letters in their box.

Sorting through them as he began his return to their apartment, one letter stopped him in his tracks. He immediately saw the return address. Msgr. R. A. Broydick. The stamping said it was mailed Saturday, two days before his death.

As he went inside, Nolan's heart was beating wildly. He was sure the monsignor had spoken to his sister, and this letter was meant to inform him of what he found out, evidence for or against his theory, possibly an angry tirade for suggesting the theory in the first place – and perhaps the last written words of a man two days away from being killed in a violent and tragic accident.

Trying to hide any sign of his apprehension, Nolan gave the mail that was not his to Sheenagh then went back to his desk. He took a deep breath and carefully opened the envelope, drawing out a handwritten letter of several pages.

Dear John,

I've chosen to write because these are things I can't speak about in person due to my state of mind. Clarity for me comes best in the written word.

In regards to the suspicions you have concerning my sister and the fire, you first need some background to understand things.

As a young man, as is true with most priests, I was idealistic and sometimes immodestly so. When my mother died, I proudly gave my entire monetary inheritance to the building fund for St. Mary's and the Rectory, and as with most things done out of excessive pride, it was in good part a mistake. Selflessness can deny the self and the rights and needs of the self.

Ten years ago, when I first entered my sixties but with no immediate plans to retire, I met with two men of the local chapter of the benevolent society that pensions priests in the Catholic Church. They assured me that both my sister, who has been my housekeeper for these 25 years, and myself would receive pensions when we retired, naming a respectable figure for me and then half that for my sister. The word of these men stayed with me these last 10 years and consoled me as I grew older.

However, I will be seventy in two months and my physical aches and pains have been telling me lately that it is close to that time.

Three weeks ago I again went to the board of the benevolent society to inform them of my plans to retire. However, none of the men I spoke to a decade earlier are still on the board. After looking through my records, I was informed by this new group that I would receive an amount considerably less than what I had been promised earlier and that my sister would receive only half of her figure. When I told them of the earlier promise, they acted as if it was unbecoming of a priest to protest their decision, that one's vow of poverty should prohibit it.

I was dumbfounded. To have given so much to my Church and to be treated this way in the end upset me greatly and threw me into a panic.

If I should die, my sister wouldn't receive any part of my pension and she would have nothing for herself aside from the small amount of money they are willing to grant her. She's always been a somewhat difficult person, not making many friends among my clerical brethren, and I'm not sure the Church will allow her to remain at the

Rectory as housekeeper to the new Rector. Thus, she would be out on the street and nearly destitute.

So I was faced with a decision of what to do, one that consumed me for days. Unfortunately, in a moment of terrible weakness and of great darkness in my soul, I decided on the plan to cause a fire in the Rectory library to cover the removal of the painting and then to claim the insurance money. My sister had no knowledge of this. I made sure the door to the library was closed and expected the fire wouldn't move beyond that room, which it didn't. I put the things I wanted to burn close to the curtains. However, as you guessed, out of some uncertainty, I did remove the photographs in the sitting room, as well as other personal items, and put them in storage in the Church basement. You're a good detective, John.

As for the painting, I did sell it the following day although it was mine to sell. That was not my crime. The fire was. But in succeeding days, I did begin to feel pangs of conscience about also trying to collect the insurance money for it. As it turned out, though, I didn't need it. What I received for the painting paid for the new residence I bought for my sister. So I chose to refuse the insurance money for the Raphael.

As for the person who bought the painting, I won't reveal who it was, but I will say that he fully believed I had stolen it. I did not use my real name nor wear any clerical clothing when I visited him in New Jersey, so he doesn't know who I am. In fact, once he looked the painting over, he told me not to give him my real name anyway, indicating his conspiracy in the matter. He bought the painting thinking it could be sold for many many times more than he paid me, and after visiting a bank while I waited in his office, he paid me in cash. It was with that money that I bought my sister's new home, putting the deed in her name. Again, it was my money and there was nothing illegal in the sale of the painting or the purchase of the home.

I'll end this letter with a plea for mercy, a plea that I hope appeals to your Christian heart and compassion.

You have all the right in the world to take this letter to the police and to the insurance company to proclaim my guilt. However, I'm hoping I'm already dead as you read this, so I'm asking you to consider not revealing its contents to anyone, to letting the matter die on its own. My parishioners would be

destroyed should they find out what I did, their faith in the Church undermined, and their sense that there is ultimate good in the world put in question.

John, I've come to know you as a person. Please ask yourself – is that the outcome you really want? I've already imposed a punishment on myself that is far worse than any court would inflict.

Again, I ask for you to exercise compassion as you decide what to do.

> **With all sincerity and love everlasting,**
> **Msgr. Robert A. Broydick.**

As he came to the end of the letter, Sheenagh entered from the kitchen. "John, I need to go to the market. Can you come with me?"

He nodded distractedly as he gazed at the pages in his hand.

"Who's the letter from?"

"No one," he said, returning it to the envelope. "From someone about business."

"What's his case about?"

"He, uh, he just wants a favor."

"Will he pay you?"

"No."

"You know we can't afford that, John. We talked about this."

"I know."

"So what are you going to do?"

He sighed and was quiet for a moment.

"John?"

"Nothing. I'm going to do nothing." With that, he put the envelope face down atop a stack of letters he was done with, letters that would soon be filed in the bottom drawer of his desk, letters that would likely never be looked at again.

THE END

Clifford Hughes

Bridget Hughes

Det. Capt. Keyes

Det. Jack Baker

A DEATH THREAT FOR MR. HUGHES

Dec. 11, 1915

Mr. C.E. Hughes,

Did we not warn you? Did you think we were not serious? We knew the route your son goes home from school. Did he not have a white chalk mark on the back of his jacket when he got home yesterday? Who do you think put it there? Do you not think it could have been a knife instead that marked up your son?

If you care about your life and the life of your family do what we asked. Give up on your run for congress. No one wants you and your cowardly pacifist opinions in our goverment. The time for that is past. War is what is needed now.

The next time we have to take action your son will be dead. You will be dead. Your wife will be dead. Your bodies will be rotting and the war with Germany will start anyway. So why try to stop it? Be smart.

        THE FIGHTERS FOR AMERICA

"Did you save the envelope this came in?"

"Right here. It came in two envelopes this morning. The smaller one, which had the letter in it, was inside, like a wedding invitation." He handed them to John Nolan.

On the face of the smaller one, in handwritten, capital letters, was this: A DEATH THREAT FOR MR. HUGHES. The larger envelope was typewritten and had no return address.

"And you said this is the second letter you received," Nolan said. "Do you still have —"

"I'll get it."

Clifford Hughes went to a mahogany sideboard and searched in a drawer. They were in the parlor of Hughes' residence on Cranberry Street in Brooklyn Heights late on a Saturday afternoon.

It was nearing sunset and the light in the room was failing, so Hughes turned on an electric lamp and resumed his search. Nolan knew enough about furniture to know that nothing in the room was from this century, other than the ceiling-high Christmas tree in the corner. Two leather wing chairs, a matching sofa, oil paintings of noble ancestors on the walls (including one of Hughes himself). Oddly out of place in a room, where all the wood and fabrics were dark, was the rug fashioned from a white polar bear skin in front of the fireplace, the massive head and yellowing teeth intact.

Nolan had a chance to study Hughes now. Late forties or early fifties, he estimated. Tall, balding, and adding weight around his middle that embarrassed him, judging by the overly loose suit jacket. He was probably a rounder and ladies' man when young, Nolan guessed, and, judging by the waxed mustache, lavender necktie, and matching pocket handkerchief, he still thought of himself that way.

"Can I ask why you didn't call the police instead of me?" Nolan asked.

Hughes was still sorting through the drawer. "What do you know about me?"

"I know you're against America entering the war. And I know you're running for a seat in Congress."

"A seat representing Brooklyn. And it would be the Brooklyn police who would investigate, men who are getting paid off by our current congressman, the man I'm trying to replace. So I wanted a private detective."

"How did you get my name?"

"I asked around. People had good things to say about you. By the way, I have to speak at the garment workers' conference at Madison Square Garden over in Manhattan in a couple of hours. Can you —"

"I brought my revolver. I can go with you." Nolan said. He examined the letter again. "Did your son actually have a chalk mark on his jacket when he got home yesterday? Can I see it?"

Hughes turned toward the stairs and shouted. "Bridget! Please come down here! And bring Tom's jacket with you, but don't touch the chalk spot!"

Nolan had his back to the staircase, but in a moment, he could hear footsteps. He rose from the chair and turned.

"This is my wife, Bridget. Dear, this is John Nolan, the detective I mentioned. Let's have that jacket, if you will. And where did you put that first letter?"

She handed the jacket to him, went over to the side-

board, shooed her husband aside, and opened a different
drawer.

Nolan guessed she was no older than himself and he
was only twenty-eight. A beautiful girl. Her hair was
bobbed, a fashion he had begun to see on women
strolling on Fifth Avenue, and she wore a beaded ban-
deau across her forehead, another fashion growing
popular.

She handed the letter to her husband. "I should think
we would want to throw that jacket out," she said.

Southern Ireland, Nolan knew immediately. To
Americans, the various accents were all Irish. To him and
anyone else from Ireland, they were all regional.

"Won't we need this as evidence?" Hughes asked
Nolan. "Can you people get fingerprints off fabric?"

"No," Nolan said. "But maybe there's something in the
dust a chemist can find. Looks like plaster dust from
here."

"Mr. Nolan, you're from Ireland," Mrs. Hughes
observed with delight.

"County Carlow."

"County Waterford," she said, beaming with pride.

Nolan was aware of something in her husband's face
just then, a flash of jealousy. His much younger wife –
there was already a tension there. Add to it a man her
own age, an Irishman, and decent looking. Yes, Nolan
knew he had to be careful.

Perhaps Mrs. Hughes saw the same thing. She turned
and went back up the stairs.

Hughes handed him the letter. As with the other one,
there were two envelopes. The smaller envelope, with the
same threatening phrase on it, contained the folded letter.

Dec. 7, 1915

Mr. C.E. Hughes,
    We read in the newspapers you are running for
congress. A bad idea, you stinking pacifist. We
will kill you and your family unless you state
in public in the next two days that you've
changed your mind. If you don't like war then
don't let the war be on you and your family.
        THE FIGHT FOR AMERICA

"It looks like the same paper, the same typewriter. The d's and b's are all filled in," Nolan said. "Different post-marks, though. Westhampton and Manorville. Aren't they both out on Long Island?"

"On the eastern half of the island, yes."

"I'll have to take these to get them photographed."

Hughes had a nautical map of Long Island rolled out on a side table. Nolan glanced at it. The island was larger than he expected. It had to be a hundred miles end to end.

"What do you think?" her husband asked. "Are these men serious? Would they harm my family?"

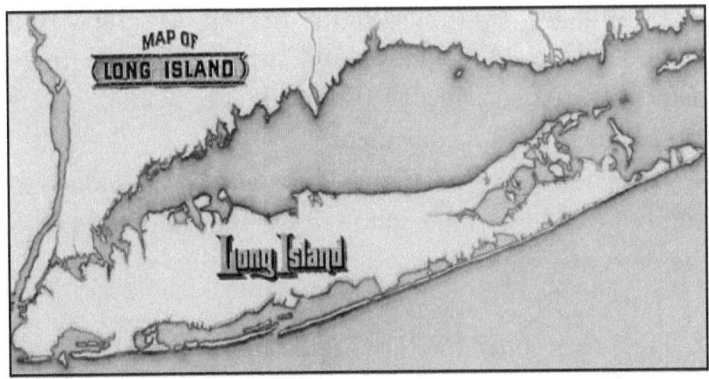

"First, I don't think there are men behind this – just one man. In the first letter you showed me, he signed it 'The Fighters for America.' In this letter, it's 'The Fight for America.' My guess is he invented this group to sound more threatening. But it's just a guess."

"But even if it's one man, would he harm my family?"

Nolan knew to be cautious. "If there's a chance he would – and I would say there's a chance – then you have to treat it as if he *would* harm your family."

Hughes sighed and massaged his temples with the flattened palms of his hands, something Nolan had seen him do several times during their meeting. "I guess this is one of those moments."

Nolan waited. "What do you want to do, sir?"

Hughes' expression hardened and he slowly shook his head. "I can't back down. I can't let the warmongers win."

They quickly put together a plan. Nolan would hire three bodyguards, one each for Hughes, his wife, and his son starting Monday morning. That would free him to find the man – or men, if that was the case – threatening them.

As Hughes dressed upstairs for his speech, Nolan used the parlor's private telephone to call the Pinkerton National Detective Agency and arrange for the three detectives. (Nolan employed no one else, working alone out of his Brooklyn apartment.)

As he hung up, the Hughes' son, who Nolan judged to be about eight or nine, came down the stairs. "Are you the detective?" he asked.

"I am."

The boy stepped forward and boldly offered his hand.

"I'm Tom. Do you have a revolver? Can I see it?"

"I can't let you handle it, but this is it." Nolan drew it from his shoulder holster beneath his jacket.

"Is it a Colt? That's the one I want to get."

"Smith and Wesson."

"Wyatt Earp used a single action Colt."

Nolan had to smile as the front doorbell rang. He told the boy he ought to go back upstairs. Once he did, Nolan, with his revolver still out, went to answer it, keeping the gun behind his back. It was the chauffeur for the automobile that had been sent by the garment workers to pick up Hughes. A green Winton touring car was idling at the curb.

Hughes appeared from behind Nolan, wearing a top hat and tailcoat and carrying a cane. An elegant sight, Nolan thought, something for the garment workers to be proud of.

Once in the motor and on their way over the Brooklyn Bridge into Manhattan, Hughes asked Nolan what his stance was on the European war.

"I don't have one. Being Irish and Catholic, I had my problems with the English when it began. If Germany took a step into Ireland, though, I'd be keen on the fight."

"Of course, that's the real test for a pacifist," Hughes said. "What do you do if an army invades your country? Switzerland, in my opinion, is doing the right thing by staying neutral and letting Germany in. If an army marches in and you don't fight back, nothing happens. No one dies. Life goes on as usual. At worst, there's a new ruling government faced with the same problems as before – keeping the lights on, keeping the garbage picked up, keeping crime down."

"He's very right," the driver said.

Nolan detected a German accent.

Hughes leaned forward. "Sir, are you of German ancestry?"

"Yes, I'm proud to say. I was born in Bavaria, but I've filed my citizenship papers here."

"Then let me ask you. If you were a German soldier and you reached the United States shores and no one raised a rifle against you, what would happen?"

"Nothing. I would march over to the Schnitzel Haus on West 44th and order my lunch."

—◆—

Hughes' name was prominent nationally at that moment. A month earlier, Henry Ford, the automobile manufacturer and a fierce opponent of America entering the war, chartered an ocean liner, the *Oscar II*, and invited leading pacifists from around the United States to join him on a mission to Europe to negotiate for peace. He reasoned the professionals had been unable to, so let the amateurs, mere private citizens, try.

Helen Keller, an outspoken pacifist, and Thomas Edison declined the invitation, but several dozen lesser known figures accepted. Hughes, who was a member but not an official of the Manhattan chapter of the League for World Peace, was not invited.

However, on Dec. 4, the liner, nicknamed the "peace ship" by the press, readied to set sail from Hoboken, New Jersey, when Hughes and seven other pacifists from around the Northeast arrived at the pier. Before a crowd of newspapermen and motion picture cameras, they announced their intention to run for congressional seats in their districts to unseat men who were supporters of

America's entry into the war. ("We hope to tip the balance in Congress toward continuing neutrality," Hughes stated.)

In the *Brooklyn Daily Eagle* the next day, Hughes garnered as much attention as Ford and his ship.

Now the National Garment Workers Association, conferencing in New York City, was going to vote on whether the United states should begin preparing for war.

There was a massive crowd outside Madison Square Garden as their automobile arrived. The Garden was packed and temporary wooden podiums were being set up on nearby corners along Madison Avenue for secondary speakers to address the overflow. Hundreds of police reserves there scattered on the streets to keep order.

The featured speaker for pacifism, and the reason for the massive crowds, was ex-secretary of state William Jennings Bryan. Arriving in a Packard just ahead of them, Bryan could not open his door, the mob was so large and immovable. Hughes and Nolan actually got on the sidewalk first but could not get through the crowd to the Garden's entry.

Suddenly, a gunshot rang out, its piercing sound standing out above the dull roar of the crowd. Nolan grabbed Hughes and shoved him down onto the sidewalk, but he was afraid to draw his own revolver for fear of being mistaken for the shooter. Then there was shouting and a general commotion in two spots about fifteen feet from him, a fight in one spot and what appeared to be a bleeding man down on the sidewalk in the other. Police officers rushed in, roughly shoving people out of the way to reach both. Nolan saw an opening to the Garden's entry and pushed Hughes toward it.

"This man is Clifford Hughes, one of the speakers," he shouted at the guard.

As they were let by, Nolan glanced back in time to see a man being dragged to a police wagon at the curb.

Inside, the stage had been divided by a thick blue ribbon down the middle – one side for those "for" the question, the other for those "against." Reaching the platform, they were told a man had been shot on the sidewalk, not Bryan, but that Bryan decided to return to his hotel, fearing assassination.

"That won't make these crowds happy," one of the organizers told them. "Mr. Hughes, you're going to have to carry the flag to stop the militarists."

Hearing this, several women on the pacifists' side of the stage moved in around Hughes, filling him with ideas to present. Hughes removed his top hat and dutifully listened, earnestly nodding and jotting down suggestions on a program handed to him as each woman pressed in to have her say.

Seeing police officers swarming the stage, some with revolvers drawn, Nolan tapped Hughes on the shoulder.

"Sir, if you feel safe here, I'm going to the police station to see if the man they took away was the man sending you the death threats."

It was more than a ten-block walk to the East 22nd Street Station and the icy wind that blew through the streets quickly made Nolan miserable.

Once at the station, Nolan approached the shift captain and showed his detective's badge.

"The man I was hired to protect may have been the real target of the assassin you brought in."

The captain, reading a newspaper, his feet on his desk, said nothing. He pointed down a hallway.

Outside an interrogation room, three police detectives were about to go in.

Nolan told them about the threatening letters. "Hughes was standing only a few feet away from the man who was shot. I was wondering, if you're going to sweat this suspect, if I could listen in to figure out if you've gotten the man what's sending the letters."

When there was no answer, Nolan reached into his pocket and found three quarters. Holding them in his open palm, they were quickly confiscated.

Inside, an unshaven man, perhaps in his forties, sat in his underwear on a wooden chair in the middle of the gray cement floor, his hands and legs shackled. The room had one tiny window that no man could possibly fit through, and it was wide open, letting in the frigid December air. There were four overhead lights, placed at an angle, all bare bulbs operated with their own pull strings, and all four were on, creating a stark, glaring, white light focused on the suspect.

The detectives stood in a tight circle around him while Nolan remained in a corner.

"Hillquit. That's your name, isn't it?"

"I told you. It's Bickel."

"Well, it isn't. You had your union card on you. Local 168 of the Butchers' Union. You answer honestly or this is going to be a night you'll remember, Hillquit. The man you shot, Schmittberger, he's in the hospital surgery right now and he could die. Before he passed out, he said he thinks he was your landlord."

"I never met him in my life. He's mistaken. It's 'cuz I

look like a lot of people. I told the bluecoats that grabbed me, it was an accident my pistol went off. I just carry it for personal protection. You know how New York is. I thought the police guards at the door would take it away, so I was putting it in my boot to hide it when it went off."

The rapid-fire questions moved from one detective to another as they leaned in over Hillquit. Where are you employed? Where do you live? Are you married? Have you ever been arrested? Have you spent time in prison?

Hillquit maintained a defiant scowl, but the room was so cold and the lights so bright that he was fighting the conditions as much as the detectives. Nevertheless, he could not be moved off his story.

Nolan stepped forward. "Detectives, can I ask a question, if you don't mind?"

Reluctantly, they let him into the circle.

"Mr. Hillquit, you said you recently moved to a new apartment on 101st Street. Why did you leave your old apartment on 109th?"

"My wife and I, we just decided to leave."

"No one just decides to leave. They have a reason."

"I guess we didn't like it."

"You said you lived there two years. After two years, you woke up one morning and suddenly decided you didn't like it? You got evicted, didn't you?"

Hillquit stared at him, not answering.

Nolan leaned in on him. "You got evicted because you couldn't pay the rent. Isn't that right?"

"I admit, I had some trouble. I'm a horse butcher but they aren't butchering so many horses anymore so my paychecks is spotty."

Nolan continued. "Who owns that building on 109th

Street?"

"I don't know. I think the bank."

"No, they don't. Remember, the address of the 109th Street apartment was on your union card. Just before we came in here, I went downstairs into the basement to the police records room and looked up that property. I know who owns it. I know exactly who owns it."

Again, Hillquit just stared at him, then subtly his mouth began to tremble. "He didn't give me no damn warning. He just showed up with two men and throwed all our belongings out on the sidewalk."

The detective next to Nolan turned to him and whispered. "What records room in the basement?"

"Tell them, Mr. Hillquit. Tell them who owns it."

"Schmittberger owns it," he admitted, then began to sob.

Afterward, out in the hallway, one of the detectives congratulated Nolan.

"I just took a guess," Nolan said. "I got lucky."

"Well, I'll do you a favor then. The man you're guarding – Hughes. When I first got on the force a couple of decades ago, I was stationed in the Tenderloin, and several times we swept the brothels and he ended up in the net we threw out. I think he was in college at the time. You won't find it in the arrest reports, though, 'cuz someone higher up got paid off each time to keep it out. So I'm just telling you. Your man's no saint."

—◆—

Returning to Madison Square Garden, Nolan reached the stage after the speeches had concluded. In a shrill, resounding voice, an organizer was explaining to the 12,000 garment workers in the seats that the vote would be postponed a day to give Bryan a chance to publish his arguments in the newspapers for them to read.

As the conference broke up, women on the stage crowded around Hughes. ("A triumph, Mr. Hughes." "Memorable as anything Bryan could have said." "You struck a blow for pacifists.")

"Sir," Nolan said to him as they moved to the exit. "The man police arrested was not the man sending the letters. He was after someone else, not you."

Hughes only shrugged, apparently too dazed by the evening's experience to be concerned.

In the Winton, returning to Brooklyn with the same German driver, Hughes was silent, gazing out the window at the twinkling skyline of Manhattan as they crossed the bridge.

"You know, history is quite a thing," he finally said. "You aren't even aware that you're making history as you're making it. Your only thought is to do the right thing with no thought of the acclaim it will bring you. For

The Brooklyn Bridge at night

me, the only thing that mattered tonight was to say the things that needed so badly to be said."

Reaching his townhouse in Brooklyn Heights, Hughes instructed the driver to take Nolan on to his residence. Then, ebulliently, he tipped him a full dollar.

When Hughes was safely inside, the German leaned over the back seat. "Where to, sir?"

"Still in Brooklyn. Clinton Avenue at Fulton. You know where it is?"

"I know where's it is. What part of Ireland you from?"

"A village no one's heard of southwest of Dublin."

"If my Germans march into Ireland, I'll tell them to leave your little town alone."

They drove the ten minutes in an awkward silence. Nolan felt for coins in his pocket for a tip but realized he had none left. He was not about to give away a dollar, though, especially to a man who apparently made more money than him as a chauffeur for rich men.

As they drove, the neighborhoods grew seedier and the townhouses became tenements. Christmas wreaths on doors became less frequent.

"This is good enough. You can let me out at the corner."

As he exited, Nolan leaned back in the door. "I'm going to be honest. I've tipped myself out of coins tonight. I have nothing left. Sorry. It has nothing to do with you being German."

The driver smirked as he drove away. Maybe they won't leave my town alone after all, Nolan thought.

He walked the half block to his building. Many of the gas street lights were broken – boys continually threw stones at them – so he became keenly aware of what may be in the shadows. During the day, with so many people on the street, men going to work, women going to market, children playing, his was a relatively safe district. However, at night, in this and any other neighborhood in Brooklyn, there was danger. Nolan checked the revolver in his shoulder holster.

Construction debris lay outside his building, barely leaving him a path to the door. New York City was rapidly modernizing and even his district was seeing changes. His building was going through a renovation, with bathrooms and kitchen sinks with running water being added to each apartment. The work in his apartment had been completed in July, giving him a feeling of Fifth Avenue luxury compared to what he was used to. In every tenement in New York City he had lived in until then, all the apartments on a floor shared one bathroom and one cold water spigot in the common hallway.

Inside, he stood still in his living room and listened. Could he hear Sheenagh breathing in the bedroom? His wife was nearly three months pregnant and recently, when she slept, her breath would come in short wheezes.

Her pregnancy had become difficult in recent weeks. She had trouble sleeping through the night, she cried for little reason, and the "baby sickness" had begun early. She was a beautiful girl, but there was a haggard quality in her face lately, and Nolan noticed she would not look at her own reflection in the bathroom mirror, averting her eyes, when they were in there together.

He undressed in the living room, carried his clothes into the bedroom, and quietly slipped into bed. The moment he did, though, Sheenagh got out and rushed to the bathroom. He followed. She was bent over the toilet but made no motion to be sick.

He waited a few moments. "Sheenagh, are you all right?"

"Go back to bed."

He waited a bit and still she was not sick. Nolan put his arms around her while she was still bent over.

"I'm so miserable," she said.

"There's a point to this. A baby."

"Six more months of this, though."

"Your cousin said the sickness came and went with her."

"It doesn't for everyone."

She suddenly pushed him away and bent lower over the toilet but was not immediately sick.

"Please, John, go back to bed."

He waited a moment, feeling a wave of compassion for her, but decided she would only feel worse if he was standing there watching when she finally was sick. So he went in to sleep.

Nolan was waiting outside Hughes' townhouse at seven o'clock Monday morning. Only two Pinkerton men appeared, though. The third was delayed until noon, he was told.

The two who did show up were both large men, well over six feet tall and heavyset, evidently hired as body-guards by Pinkerton for their size. Nolan was five feet nine, so as they stood on the sidewalk, they towered over him.

"Here are your assignments," he said. "I want —"

"I don't knows if I like some little Irishman giving me orders," the smaller of the two said. "I was told Mr. Hughes hired us. Just who the hell are you?"

Nolan stayed quiet a moment as they stared at each

other. "I was the one who hired you."

"So you're paying our bills, Mick?"

"That's none of your business, but I made the call to Pinkerton. I already work for Mr. Hughes."

The larger of the two tapped the other detective's arm. "Let'em be. All right, captain, what do you want us to do."

Inside, the three met with the family. Tom left for school with his guard, Mrs. Hughes left with her guard to shop in Manhattan, and Nolan was told he would accompany Hughes to a meeting of a peace group in the neighborhood.

"I've got to change first," Hughes, who was still in his bathrobe, told him. "Why don't you wait in the parlor."

As he walked about the parlor, he began to dwell on the detective's insults to him, something he had warned himself not to do. Insults like that could fester dangerously in one's thinking. Anti-Irish feeling was rampant in New York as were feelings against the Italians, the Jews, the Germans, the French. One group hated another. Us and them. It was a thinking that was like an infectious disease, like cholera or tuberculosis.

When he and Sheenagh had gone in search of an apartment, if they found something that appealed to them, they always made sure to go around and knock on the doors of other tenants in the building, to get a sense of whether, as an Irish family, they would be welcome. The apartment they finally chose was in a tenement where the families were Irish, Jewish, Hungarian, Greek, Russian, and French-Canadian. They hoped so many differences would draw the families closer together – and it had.

Indeed, Nolan did not want to be first and foremost Irish. He wanted to be American. He took pains not to dress so much like an Irishman, with his trousers high off the boot, and to not talk so much like an Irishman, extravagantly rolling his R's. However, his accent was impossible to hide completely.

On a parlor table, Nolan found the previous day's Sunday editions of the *Times*, The *World*, and the *Herald* on the sofa. The Madison Square Garden conference was on the front page of each. However, Bryan's aborted speech, printed in its entirety, was featured in each, not Hughes' speech, only portions of which managed to find their way into the stories.

Hughes came down in a morning coat and top hat as Nolan was reading the papers.

"Sir, it's a shame more isn't said about your speech."

"Bryan's speech would have been eloquent," Hughes said, putting on his overcoat, "if he'd given the damn thing. But to push the speech that was actually delivered so far down into the story, as if it's a mere afterthought, why, that takes away from what actually happened. Bryan didn't have the courage to show up. I did. It's unfair."

The meeting was in a townhouse on the other end of Cranberry Street. The Brooklyn Chapter of Citizens Against War. As Hughes entered, the seven members who were already there, all women, stood and applauded.

"My husband and I were there last night, Clifford, and if you didn't tip the scales away from America joining this nonsense, nothing will," said the hostess, an attractive young woman, as she took their coats and hats.

They found seats while slices of fruit cake, Swedish

caraway cookies, and tea were offered by a maid. Then Hughes told of the threats to his life and the need to hire a bodyguard, which brought solemn, admiring gazes from the women to both Hughes and Nolan.

"Clifford, dear," said an elderly woman whose hand had been cupped about her ear, to improve her hearing, since they entered. "I couldn't be there last night. So might you tell me the main point you made, if you don't mind?"

Hughes cleared his throat briefly as he thought. Then, with a theatrical air, he slowly rose. "It was just this ... I said I'm wholeheartedly against preparation for this war in any form. That's because preparing for war *is* war. No man ever armed himself with a knife and fork unless he was about to attack a steak or chop of some kind. If America decides to arm herself, we know what we will get – the same as the Europeans are getting. Devastation and death. Tragedy and tribulation."

He spoke for another ten minutes, his voice becoming more confident, his delivery more dramatic. Nolan was suspicious of orators generally, of the spell they can cast on ignorant men. Nevertheless, he found himself drawn in by Hughes. There were causes worth being inspired by, he knew – the excessive wealth of some and the grim poverty of most, the abuses of the working man by the industrial robber barons.

He wondered: Was Hughes right? Should America stay out of this war?

As he listened, he found himself admiring Hughes, the kindness in his face, the earnestness in his voice, the decency and clear thinking in his words. Certainly, strong principles must lie behind all that, Nolan thought.

The great men in American life, the ones who steered
the course of history – Teddy Roosevelt, Henry Ford,
Samuel Gompers, Albert Einstein. Perhaps Hughes was a
man about to become one of them. Nolan wondered if,
in another six months, he would be telling people, "Yes, I
know Mr. Hughes very well. I've been to his home and
met his wife. A great man."

When Hughes finished, applause again broke out, with
Nolan joining it. Then the women rose and closed in
around Hughes, who kept a grim expression as he accepted their adulation.

Later, Nolan and Hughes met the third Pinkerton man
at Hughes' residence, so Nolan was free to spend the
afternoon researching at the Brooklyn Public Library.

Reaching the library, he began with *Who's Who in
America*. Their most recent edition was from 1910, a mas-
sive, red, leather-bound book of nearly 3,000 pages.
Initially, he thought he found Hughes' entry.

**Hughes, C. F. Charles, Lawyer and
Statesman. Born, Brooklyn, N.Y.,
1841.**

The date stopped him. This must be Hughes' father,
he realized. There was no entry for the son.

The father had been a congressman from Brooklyn,
serving on the House Committee on Naval Affairs, before
being appointed Assistant Secretary of the Navy.

Now his son was a leading pacifist and running for one
of the other Brooklyn seats in Congress. Interesting,
Nolan thought.

In recent copies of the *Brooklyn Daily Eagle*, he found
several letters to the editor railing against pacifists, but he

would need to see the original letters to say if the type matched those sent to Hughes, photographs of which he brought with him.

At the *Eagle*'s Johnson Street office, Nolan bribed the chief archivist with a quarter to see the published letters file as well as the Clifford Hughes file.

Finding the letters against pacifism, he placed them against the photographs. In the death threats, the d's and b's were filled in consistently, but the a's and o's were not. None of the typed letters matched.

In Hughes file, there were more than twenty clippings. The earliest were society page mentions of him attending Yale in the fall of 1888, then Dartmouth in the fall of 1889. However, there was no mention of a graduation until 1894 – a degree in history from Rutgers College in New Jersey. Was he kicked out of the first two?

Then the clippings skipped more than a decade. In 1912, his father died while still serving in Congress. Apoplexy struck him at breakfast. All the other clippings were dated between the summer of 1914 and the present, and all concerned the younger Hughes' association with the pacifist movement.

Returning the files, Nolan left the *Eagle*'s office and took a trolley home. Unable to find a seat, he stood against a door, his breath steaming in the December chill. Many people carried wrapped Christmas gifts and had smiles on their faces. Even with war looming, the spirit of the holidays could not be dampened. Fortunately, his shopping for Sheenagh was done. Leather gloves, three gold leaf picture frames, and new kitchen knives.

As the trolley bounced along, he considered everything he had learned about this case. He did not know what to think exactly about the European war, but he had met enough pacifists to know most were idealists – misguided maybe, but idealists. Perhaps Hughes had been a rounder when young, but he married, had a child, and had now developed character and principles. Indeed, reckless boys sometimes became the most responsible of men.

Reaching his apartment door late in the afternoon, Nolan tried his key but found it was already unlocked. Once inside, he heard voices in the kitchen.

Sheenagh, still in her bathrobe, was sitting at the kitchen table, drinking coffee. A well-dressed woman sat opposite her, with her back to Nolan. However, the woman turned when he entered. It was Mrs. Hughes. She was wearing pearl earrings and a beige sweater suit with a band of fur at the bottom.

"Here you are," Mrs. Hughes said rising. "I came by thinking this was your office and it's not. It's your home. And you didn't tell me you had a beautiful wife, John."

Sheenagh was not happy about her being there, her look to Nolan said.

"No, I didn't," he said. "But Mrs. Hughes, we've talked only one time, if you recall."

"It's Bridget, please. Your wife is so lovely, John. And a baby on the way. You didn't tell me that either."

"Again, we've only spoken once, and it was just to say a few words. Can I ask why you're here?"

"Well, you see, it's my bodyguard. I've decided I want him changed."

"What's wrong with him?"

"If I'm going to spend the entire day with him, he should be a man who can talk a bit, hold a conversation. Your man is very cold. He does his job all right, I suppose, but I need to talk to the people I'm with. That's just the kind of person I am."

"He's a Pinkerton man and very experienced."

"Well, can't we get a Pinkerton man who's talkative?"

"If he's doing his job properly, he should be paying attention to other things."

"He can talk and look for danger at the same time, can't he?" She raised her cup to Sheenagh as if indicating to a maid she wanted more coffee. "I was thinking, though. I want to become involved in this, in protecting my family, so perhaps I'll hire the bodyguards myself."

"Don't you want to talk to Mr. Hughes first? And where is your bodyguard right now?"

Sheenagh refilled her cup.

"He's out in my Packard, waiting. I ordered him to stay there, and I can tell you he wasn't happy about it. But my husband would say just what I'm saying, which is that you want to feel comfortable around a person you're going to spend all day with. I want to have a role in this and that'll be my role, choosing the bodyguards. That's settled then." She turned to Sheenagh. "Can I ask, dear, how did you catch our John?"

Sheenagh looked insulted. "I didn't catch *our John*. If anything, he caught me."

Nolan quickly jumped in. "We met in grammar school. We caught each other, to be honest."

"I didn't mean anything by it, dear. That came out wrong. He's the lucky one, I'm sure."

"How did you meet your husband, Mrs. Hughes?" Nolan asked.

"It's Bridget. I was the girl who cared for his sister's children."

"I'm sure many young Irishmen would have knocked on your door, if you'd let them," Nolan said.

"I'm sure there would have been dozens of them, if I'd been looking in that direction. But to be truthful, when I arrived in America, I became engaged to an Irish boy. He couldn't find proper work for a long time, though, and I guess I ran out of patience with him."

"Where is he now?" Nolan asked.

"I heard he lives in Hartford and is married, probably to a good Irish girl because that's the way he is."

"No regrets ... for not waiting a bit longer?" Sheenagh asked.

"I don't regret anything, dear, and I would advise you should follow the same prescription. Yes, my husband is quite a bit older, but when I first met him, he swept me off my feet. My Irish boy had no chance from that moment on."

Mrs. Hughes stood and picked up her white ermine fur coat off the back of the chair. "Sheenagh, it was lovely meeting you. And John, we'll talk some other time. You can tell me more of the things you haven't told me about yourself."

She shook both their hands with an exaggerated show of familiarity, as if they were longtime friends.

When she was gone, Sheenagh put the coffee cups in the sink and silently ran the water on them.

"I'm sorry about that," he said.

"About what?"

"I gave her husband my business card. That must be how she got our address."

Her back was to him, but Nolan could tell she had begun to cry by the way her shoulders were subtly heaving. He came from behind and put his arms around her.

"Honestly, Sheenagh. I spoke two words to her in my life. She asked where I was from. I told her with her husband standing right there, and that was all."

"That's not why I'm crying. I look awful. I feel awful. I was sick twice this morning and I haven't bathed. Then she comes in here, dressed the way she was ... Oh, God."

She turned into him, and Nolan, his arms around her, let her cry, slowly rocking her until, standing at the sink, she nearly fell asleep in his arms.

By the following morning, Mrs. Hughes had hired her own bodyguard and dismissed the Pinkerton man.

Nolan spent much of the day contacting each of the seven pacifists who had joined Hughes in announcing their candidacies, men whose districts were in Pennsylvania, Ohio, and Michigan. He learned that all had received death threats, and after he described the peculiarities of the typewriter to them, especially the filled-in d's and b's, it was clear all the letters were sent by the same writer. In addition, all the letters had been mailed from the same post office in Westhampton on Long Island on the same day.

However, only Hughes was threatened a second time and that letter was sent from Manorville, about ten miles from Westhampton. Both towns were nearly sixty miles from Brooklyn.

The man was from Long Island, Nolan was sure, but it was not likely that he was from either Westhampton or Manorville. His intent was to disguise his address. Now, if he would only mail enough letters, by the process of elimination, Nolan might be able to figure which town was his.

In the afternoon, Nolan went to the offices in Manhattan of the *New York Times*. Without bribery, with only an explanation of the death threats and a promise of a story if a matching letter was found, he was allowed to look through the recent letters to the editor. However, in four hours of searching, he discovered no matches.

That evening, after dinner, he attempted to write out theories based on what he knew.

> **Member of militarist group supporting war or war preparedness.**
>
> **Man with grudge against Hughes. Get list from Hughes.**
>
> **Former military officer pushing for war. Privates and other lower ranks less likely.**
>
> **Owner of Long Island gun or ammunition manufacturer who would profit from war. Most likely privately owned company, small, maybe single owner. Or company that supplies the military with uniforms, canteens or such.**
>
> **English or French immigrant living on Long Island. Check British and French clubs, organizations.**

—◈—

"My son was kidnapped as he came out of his school this afternoon," Hughes said as he met Nolan at the front door. "A child! It makes me sick!"

Nolan had rushed right over after getting Mrs. Hughes' frantic call. He could see her behind her husband, crying in the dining room.

"Sir," Nolan said. "We have to call in the Brooklyn police. They have specialists in kidnapping."

"It just shows you. The warmongers, their depravity. They will descend to this. If they kill him —"

"They won't kill him, sir. They'll hold him to convince you to quit the race. Either that or for ransom. Sir, the police, we have to call them. And where is the boy's bodyguard?"

"He's in the kitchen. I already fired him, the fool. I want the Pinkerton man back. These warmongers, these bastards!"

"Sir, can I call —"

"Call whoever you have to! These damnable bastards!"

Nolan left Hughes pacing the front hallway, ranting to himself, and found the bodyguard in the kitchen. The rough-looking man, his hat in his hand, was seated. His revolver and holster were lying on the kitchen table.

The story Nolan got was this. The bodyguard had dropped the boy off at his private school at eight o'clock that morning in the Hughes' second automobile, a Dodge, then spent most of the afternoon in a saloon. At three o'clock, when he left to pick the boy up, he went to get the Dodge but found that all the tires had been punctured.

"I flagged a policeman. He got a patrol car to take me, but it was too late. The boy was kidnapped already ... Am I gonna get paid? It wasn't my fault."

"Take that up with Hughes."

Nolan called the Brooklyn police's detective bureau. Hughes agreed to stay home to meet the police while Nolan drove the Hughes' motor to the school to get more information.

The Beet's School on Pierrepont Street served the rich families of Brooklyn Heights. The story Nolan got from the principal was that the chauffeur for another family, who was waiting by the curb to pick up their son, saw Tom come out and wait for the Hughes' Dodge on the sidewalk. He knew the boy and said hello.

Then another man came up to Tom, crouched down, and talked to him. The boy willingly followed him to another car parked at the curb, a runabout, a Ford, and they drove off. About five minutes later, the police motor arrived with the bodyguard and then the commotion started.

"This other chauffeur, did he say what this man, the man with the Ford, looked like?"

"A mustache. Fifty maybe, your height maybe, a derby, black suit. He looked like any man generally."

When Nolan returned to the Hughes' townhouse, Hughes and his wife were arguing in the dining room and two police detectives were questioning the bodyguard in the kitchen.

Nolan went from the kitchen to the dining room listening. In the kitchen, the detectives had gotten the information out of the bodyguard that he had served three years for robbery upstate in Sing Sing, so they were questioning him about that and about his associates before and after prison and about where he managed to get a pistol permit. In the dining room, Hughes and his wife were arguing about how a convict had been hired to protect their son.

"He didn't put that on his application! How was I to know it?" Mrs. Hughes screamed through her tears.

"Did you ask him, for God's sake? If he had a job history – and I want to see it – there had to be a missing three years on it. Did you ask what the hell he did for those three years?"

Through all the noise, no one except the maid heard the telephone ring in the parlor. She came in to the dining room, waited for a short break in the screaming, and then tapped Hughes on the shoulder.

"Mr. Hughes, telephone."

"Not now."

She whispered something to him and he rushed to the parlor. Nolan followed and stood in the entryway.

"Hello? ... Is he all right? ... I have to go to the bank and make arrangements. Five thousand isn't ... Yes ... Just don't hurt the boy. You'll have your money, I promise ... Yes ... four o'clock, Saturday ... Yes ... But please, I beg you, you'll get the money, but don't hurt him."

The police detectives and the bodyguard had joined Nolan in the parlor entryway to listen by the time Hughes hung up.

Hughes was ashen-faced, his mouth trembling with rage. "They want a ransom. Then they'll call back Saturday at four o'clock with instructions."

The police plan was to place a detective at the telephone company's central office to trace the call. Also, a dictograph would be set up on the line coming into Hughes' home to transmit the call to another room where a stenographer could transcribe what was said. Finally, two additional lines would be added for detectives to listen in to the call.

On Saturday morning, as all this was being arranged,

an envelope arrived in the mail that Mrs. Hughes opened. Only a library card was inside – her son's library card. There was no letter with it.

"Oh, God!" she said. "Tom has a little cowboy wallet and this was in it. Does this mean they already killed him?"

One of police detectives, staying around the clock at the residence, shook his head. "No, they're just sending you proof they've got him."

In an aside, he whispered to Nolan. "If they wanted to prove they killed him, they'd of sent an eyeball pickled in vinegar."

Nolan examined the envelope. It was postmarked Yaphank, another town on Long Island.

That afternoon, as the grandfather clock in the parlor loudly clicked down to four o'clock, the somber silence in the room magnified the sound, creating a terrible tension in the house. Hughes paced distractedly by the main telephone, and two detectives stood by the added phones, ready to pick up. Nolan went into the kitchen where the stenographer was preparing to listen at the dictograph, which would allow him to hear as well.

At a minute past four, the bell on the parlor phone sounded, startling everyone.

Hughes grabbed it. "Hello?"

"Don't even bother to tell me the police aren't there. I don't care a whit if they're there or they ain't. This is what you're going to do. Are you listening?'

"I'm here."

"Are there policemen all around you, Mr. Hughes?"

"I would tell you they're not here, but you wouldn't believe me. I don't want to endanger my son, so I didn't call them."

"If that's your play, it's very wise, because if you don't do what I say, well, you know how that play will go. So listen to me. At midnight tonight, go to the Columbus Circle entrance of Central Park. A man will be there, a man what's not me. He will say, 'could be snow,' and you hand him the money in an envelope then walk away. My man will leave and if he's followed by the police or if he's picked up by them or if he don't make it back to where I am in two hours, your son will be killed. And believe me, I'll make it painful for him and for you when you hear about how I done it. Do you understand, Mr. Hughes?"

"Yes, I understand. The Columbus Circle entrance to Central Park. Midnight."

"We'll see if you understand. Once I have the money and feel safe, I'll call you Monday some time with the next instructions. One more thing. If you or some stupid bluecoat decides to follow my man in a motor, my man is instructed to look for headlamps behind him that stay with him. So don't even think about that. He'll know it's the police in that motor and you know what'll happen to your boy."

The line went dead and Hughes hung up. Nolan rushed to the parlor where the analysis was already underway. In loud voices, the two detectives traded ideas.

"Sounded American, not foreign," the older detective said.

"Didn't sound educated."

"Sounded very methodical, though. A couple of places, it sounded like he was reading, like he wrote out his speech. This man won't make many mistakes."

The plan they formulated was this. Three motors – a

runabout, a touring car, and a motor truck – would be used as a shadow detail to follow the money man once he reached his own automobile. The police motors would follow thirty yards behind him in a line but stay fifty yards apart. Every few minutes, the lead motor would pull to the side and be passed by the other two before pulling back into the line. That way, the money man would always be seeing different headlamps behind him.

The detective who had been at the central telephone office called to say the kidnapper had placed his call at a pay telephone at Grand Central Terminal in Manhattan. And because of the crowd at that time of day, it would be impossible to find someone who remembered him.

"There's one mistake he already didn't make," the older detective said.

Nolan rode with a detective named Jack Baker, ironically in a bakery delivery truck that had been confiscated by police in a tax fraud case.

By eleven o'clock, they were parked across the street from the park entrance on Central Park West in clear sight of the gates. The runabout and touring car, also confiscated vehicles, were in front of them.

Fearing the money man would be watching from inside the park gates, Nolan and Baker hunched down as far as they could in the truck's seat. However, as midnight neared, the temperature dropped sharply and snow flurries began to fall, partially obscuring their view.

"My guess is there is no second man," Nolan said. "It's all one man doing this and he'll be the one to pick up the money."

"Half the time in these situations, you're right," said

Baker, who could have passed for a college student, his face was so youthful. "But half the time you're not, so we can't take a chance and just grab him."

Suddenly, there was a knock on their window. A craggy-faced man, with a mustache so thick it covered much of his mouth, was grinning at them.

Baker rolled down the window. "Captain Keyes."

"Just wanted to know everything's all right," Keyes said. "You boys in place?"

"Yes, sir. We're ready."

The captain nodded and moved on to the runabout.

Nolan was astonished. "What the hell's he doing? If this suspect is watching, he'll know what's going on. It'll get this boy killed. Why didn't you tell him to stay away?"

Baker shook his head. "He's my boss and he'll bite your head off if you tell him something he don't like."

Eventually, the captain moved on, disappearing back up Central Park West.

At five minutes to midnight, with the snow flurries diminishing, they spotted Hughes approaching the entrance. Once there, he stood right in the gate. Then a shorter man, with his collar up and his derby pulled down tight, emerged from the shadows just inside the park. He said something to Hughes who pulled the envelope from his jacket. The man took it and walked back into the park, disappearing again into the shadows. Hughes walked away toward Broadway.

Nolan turned to Baker. "What do we do now?"

"Just wait. He'll come out sooner or later. He's not going to walk through the park to another entrance. Not in the dark, not in this city, not with $5,000 in his pocket. Just wait."

Indeed, ten minutes later, the money man re-emerged. He walked north on Central Park West, actually passing within feet of their motors. Baker and Nolan slid as low in their seats as possible. In a moment, Nolan cracked open his door and, through the snow flurries, he watched the man stop at a black Ford runabout parked at the curb a half block up the street and then glance down the sidewalk to see if he was being followed. Seeming confident, the man cranked the Ford to start the engine, then pulled into the street and passed the police motors.

"Here we go," Baker said.

Their three motors were started, and the touring car, first in line, pulled out. It followed the Ford, which had turned east on 59th Street. Their runabout and bakery truck fell in behind.

They kept their distance and changed places within a few blocks as planned. Twice the money man stuck his head out the side window to see what was trailing him, but he kept driving as if he was not suspicious.

The Ford stayed on 59th but was traveling at a very slow speed. Fearful of attracting attention, Nolan thought. He wrote down the license plate in his notebook.

"If he's going out to Long Island, watch, he'll take the Blackwell's Island Bridge," Baker said.

The Ford did, stopping to pay the dime toll. Baker, in the lead now, had to let a Chevrolet, a civilian's motor, get in between him and the Ford. Briefly, he lost the Ford when the toll man took his time lifting the gate.

On the other side of the bridge, they caught the Ford again on Jackson Avenue.

"Mr. Nolan, you work alone?" Baker asked as they settled in behind.

"I do. A one-man agency."

"You're lucky you don't have a boss. You can't tell mine nothing, so no one bothers to. At my first precinct, up in the Bronx, I had a gruff old sergeant who moved here from Canada. Was the same way. On his first night in the city, he stayed at the Manhattan Hotel on Madison Avenue and ordered a Manhattan cocktail during dinner. He liked it, so for years, wherever he lived in the city, he'd travel to that hotel to drink those Manhattans."

"You can get a Manhattan anywhere. It wasn't invented there."

"Exactly." Baker pulled to the side to let himself be passed by the two other motors. "I told him that once and he yelled at me. He said it wasn't true, that you could only get a real Manhattan cocktail at the Manhattan hotel and how could I be so stupid to not know that. Now he's retired and he lives up in Connecticut and he makes the long trip into the city a couple of times a year just to drink a Manhattan cocktail at the Manhattan Hotel."

"The police touring car is pulling off."

"I see it."

Their truck moved up in line to behind the runabout. However, the money man suddenly made a sharp left turn without signaling. And their runabout, too close behind him, skidded on the snowy street and slid hard into the curb beyond the corner. Baker managed to make the turn as did the touring car behind them.

"The Ford, it's slowing down."

They had reached the entrance ramp to the Long Island Motor Parkway, a forty-five mile toll road. Only the touring car was still with them, their runabout apparently lost for good. The parkway appeared nearly empty.

"Damn. We can't follow," Baker said.

"Why not?"

"The parkway don't allow trucks." Baker pulled to the side of the street well before the ramp, as did the touring car. One of the detectives from that motor came over and Baker rolled down his window.

"You can't go on the parkway," the detective said.

"I know that," Baker said.

"So I'd be the only one following and that's no good. It'd be just me and him and he'd figure it out ... What do you want to do?"

With the snow falling heavily, Baker, Nolan, and the detective watched the Ford go through the toll gate and move onto the parkway.

"Leave him go," Baker said. "We don't want to risk the Hughes boy."

⸻✦⸻

By eight o'clock Monday morning, December twentieth, Nolan, the team of Brooklyn detectives, as well as the dictograph and stenographer, were back in place. As they waited for the next call, the mail arrived with another letter from the kidnapper, postmarked East Moriches. This one contained only the boy's school identification card.

The first call of the day came from a precinct captain in Nassau County on Long Island. The license plate Nolan had written down belonged to a 1914 Ford runabout stolen from the parking lot of the railroad station in Hempstead.

"You gave us 54984. We know thieves will paint over a one with blue paint to make it a four, so we checked on 51981, and, yes, that one was stolen out of Hempstead."

Captain Keyes happened to be there when the call

came and he took the phone away from Hughes and identified himself.

"Captain," he said. "If you'll do me a courtesy and make a great mark in the column for yourself, we've got a boy what was kidnapped from Brooklyn in that Ford. Could you get your men out in Hempstead and go door to door looking for the auto and for the boy?"

Baker turned to Nolan and shook his head. They both knew he would not be in Hempstead. What a waste of time.

Using an atlas found in the Hughes' study and a charcoal sketching pencil the family had, Nolan and Baker

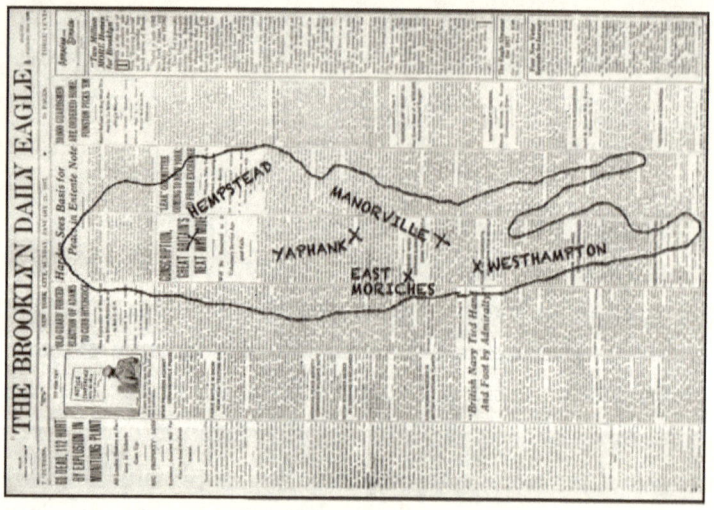

Rough map of Long Island

drew a rough map of Long Island on a sheet of the *Brooklyn Daily Eagle*.

They had four towns from which letters had been sent and they had Hempstead. However, they saw no pattern once they were all on the map. They seemed to be scattered all over the island.

The call from the kidnapper did not come until after lunch. Hughes took it.

"Mr. Hughes, you did the right thing. I have the money and your boy is still alive. Do you want him back?"

"Of course I do."

"Well, now we're back to what I asked in the first place. You and your pacifist friends have to drop out of their political races."

"You said only I had to pull out."

"Now I want all of you out, the eight of you pacifist fools."

"These men, I can't tell them to not run. These are principled men who won't do it. They won't let themselves be intimidated."

"Then you tell them I stole your boy as a warning to them all. If I can get your boy that easy, I can get their little boy, their little girl, their wife, and I can get them that easy. They're next on my list is what you tell them."

"You have to give me some time. A week at least."

"I don't have to do anything, but I will. Today's Monday. I'll give you until … next Monday, two days after Christmas. I have to see an announcement in the *New York Times* by Tuesday morning's paper after the holiday that you and all these men are dropping out. Otherwise your son dies."

With that, he hung up.

—◆—

Over the next two days, every garage and barn in Hempstead was searched for the stolen Ford, as were those in the adjoining towns. No luck.

Three new letters arrived, postmarked Brookhaven, Eastport, and Boltsville, all containing items from Tom's wallet and nothing else. That gave Nolan and Baker three new towns to add to their map, which had been tacked to an artist's easel in the dining room.

Late Wednesday afternoon, Captain Keyes stopped by and Nolan and Baker showed him their map.

"We figure these are the towns we can eliminate," Nolan said.

"You can eliminate all of Long Island," Keyes said. "I just talked to a regional man at the Federal Bureau of Investigation. He says there's a ring working the big cities in the East. They target a rich man, kidnap a relative, and demand ransom. But he's sure they're working out of Connecticut. He says these Long Island letters are just these smart fellows trying to make us look bad. They want us to waste all our time on Long Island when that's not where they are at all."

"I don't believe that, sir," Nolan said. "If these people are up in Connecticut, it would be too far for them to travel to just mail a letter. They would send the letters from the Bronx or Queens if they were trying to throw us off."

Keyes turned on him angrily. "Who cares what the hell you think? Where'd you get the idea I care what you think?"

Baker froze and Nolan knew to be quiet.

Keyes, blustering, turned to Baker. "Why's this damned Mick even talking to me? He's not in my goddam department, for God's sake!"

Baker motioned that Nolan should leave for a moment, so he went out to the kitchen. Nolan caught only bits of what was said, but Baker eventually gave him the rest. He was to stay out of the investigation and only work as the hired bodyguard for the family.

"But look," Baker said. "Anything I learn, I'll tell you, and anything you find out, you tell me. Keyes doesn't know what he's talking about."

"There's something I thought of in the kitchen," Nolan said. "If this was just a kidnapping ring, wouldn't they have taken the boy the day they put the chalk mark on his back? This man started with political reasons. He decided on kidnapping later."

Baker recognized the sense in this. "You're absolutely right. Dammit, forget Keyes and forget Connecticut. This man is on Long Island somewhere."

After Keyes left, Hughes and his wife got into an argument. Nolan was in the kitchen, eating his supper with the maids, when he heard the shouting in another room. He asked himself: Just how much bodyguarding should he do in a situation like this?

He went to the kitchen door and cracked it open. He could see into the parlor where they were.

"If you hadn't been so damned stupid —"

"Clifford, don't call me that. I've told you —"

"When you're stupid, you're stupid, and it's a fact I can't get around."

"We paid the ransom. He won't kill Tom now."

"No, he'll just want more money. These other men won't drop out of their races. I talked to most of them. My guess is Tom is as good as dead, no matter what they do."

Mrs. Hughes broke into sobs.

"Well he is," her husband said. "And if he dies, I tell you, this marriage is over."

"You're blaming me? God, Clifford!"

"Of course I'm blaming you! Haven't you been listening?"

Hughes took a vicious swing at his wife with his balled fist. She ducked out of the way, and he swung again, missing again. Just as Nolan rushed out of the kitchen to intervene, she ran from the room toward the staircase, still crying.

Ten minutes later, Hughes came into the kitchen. "John, I want a word with you."

They moved out into the hallway.

"Your revolver," Hughes said. "Can you get me one like it?"

"I could. If you're sure you want one."

"And teach me to shoot it. Damn. This is the last time anything like this is going to happen to me and I sit here helpless to do anything."

"Sir, if I can ask, if you had a revolver, how would that have changed anything?"

"I don't know, but all I know is I want one. So get me one."

Nolan watched Hughes walking away, talking to himself under his breath. He was not sure why, but it made him smile. Another insight into human beings he was never going to forget. The great pacifist. The principled man. He shook his head and went back to his dinner.

—◈—

On Christmas Eve, Friday, two more letters arrived at the Hughes residence, postmarked Speonk and Mastic. They went on the Long Island map but made the pattern of towns no less random.

Hughes decided he would stay home for the day and work on a speech, which gave Nolan a chance to go back to Brooklyn. Sheenagh had a doctor's appointment at four o'clock and he wanted to go with her.

As he traveled home on the subway, crowded with people carrying Christmas gifts, Nolan thought about the Hughes case. He realized he was beginning to fear failure, a failure that would be marked by the boy's death, perhaps by pieces of his dismembered body washing up on a Long Island beach. To that point, as a detective, he had been lucky in most of his cases. Perhaps the grim reality of detective work was finally catching up with him.

As soon as he walked in his apartment door, the telephone in the parlor began to ring. He picked up. "Nolan Detective Bureau."

"John, this is Bridget Hughes. I need you."

"Why? Has something happened?"

"Clifford won't let me leave the house without a bodyguard, and I need to go to the pharmacy just up on Fulton Street. I need some nerve pills. I can't sleep at night, and I'm upset all the time, and my doctor has sent a prescription over to them. I understand you've got our Dodge for a few days. Please, will you come by and take me?"

Nolan gritted his teeth. He knew that pharmacy. It was only a few blocks from the Hughes townhouse. The pharmacy could have a boy walk the pills over, but if he said no to her, it would likely upset her further.

"Mrs. Hughes, I could come by about three and pick you up, I suppose. Or I could pick up the pills myself and drop them off to you."

"No, I have to get out of here. I have to. Please, pick me up."

"All right. At three then. Look for me and the Dodge

outside."

Nolan hung up then glanced behind him. Sheenagh was standing in the doorway.

"Was that Mrs. Hughes?"

"Yes," he said. "She's in bad shape and needs a ride to a pharmacy to pick up some pills. I said we'd take her on the way to the doctor. I hope you don't mind."

"What time did you tell her we'd come by? At three?" She did not appear to mind at all.

"Yes, in twenty minutes, if that's all right. We'll run her to the pharmacy and home, then we'll go on to the doctor."

Sheenagh looked back at the clock in the kitchen. "I'll be ready."

Nolan went through his mail. He wrote bank checks for the telephone company and the green grocer, then prepared another invoice for Hughes for time and expenses.

Getting a drink of water at the kitchen sink, he glanced over at the clock. A quarter to three.

"Sheenagh, we've got to get going," he shouted.

"I'm ready."

Startled, he turned. She was standing right behind him.

"Oh my God." He shook his head in disbelief, then made a show of pretending to fall over.

She had on her best dress, black and white with a lacy shirtwaist. She had brushed her hair and put on makeup, including lipstick. Seeing her for the past month in little else but a bathrobe, he was astonished.

He kissed her cheek. "What a beautiful girl."

She smiled, the first time he had seen her smile in days.

"Well, dear, I'm glad I can still make you look at me. Let's get going."

When they got to Cranberry Street, Nolan pulled the motor to the curb and started to get out.

"No, I'll go," Sheenagh said, opening her door.

He suddenly knew what the dressing up had been about. He watched her go through the wrought iron gate, up the steps, and ring the doorbell. Mrs. Hughes opened the door herself and seemed to not recognize Sheenagh at first.

As the two walked to the auto, Nolan saw that Mrs. Hughes did not look well. Once they were both in the back seat, Nolan turned.

"Mrs. Hughes. Are you all right?"

"I don't sleep anymore. I was telling Sheenagh. It's the worst thing I've ever gone through. John, please, find Tom. My marriage —" She began to sob, then forced herself to stop. She dabbed at her eyes with her sleeve and Sheenagh gave her a handkerchief. "If you can't find him, I don't know what's going to happen to me."

It was dark by the time the appointment at Brooklyn Hospital ended. "She's in fine shape," was the doctor's verdict.

As they drove home, Nolan took a detour by the waterfront.

"Where are we going?" Sheenagh asked.

"A night out, if you're well enough. You deserve it."

He had seen an advertisement for a seafood restaurant that overlooked New York Harbor, the Captain's Table, that was to stay open Christmas Eve. He felt they could afford it this one time. Their waiter put candles on the table, which was by the window. As they ate – clam chowder, white fish, and crackers for her; the baked flounder for him – they watched tugs accompany one of the great liners into port under a full moon.

As they were leaving, Sheenagh stopped to chat with a waiter, and Nolan had a chance to compliment the owner, who was greeting customers as they came in.

"It was like a vacation to come here and see the harbor. Quite wonderful," Nolan told him.

"If you're interested, I just opened a new restaurant on the ocean in Patchogue on Long Island. You can reach it on a train out of Penn Station, have your meal, look at the waves, and get right back on the late train to the city. In fact, we've put all our eleven restaurants near the rail lines on Long Island and in Brooklyn. They can all be vacations for you."

The owner retrieved a handbill from behind the desk for him, showing the locations. Nolan was about to stuff it in his overcoat pocket when the map caught his eye.

Sheenagh returned and as she put on her overcoat, she saw his expression studying the handbill. "What's the matter?"

"The other restaurants the owner has on Long Island. He has them in Eastport, East Moriches, and Brookhaven. They're all on the rail lines."

"So?"

"The kidnapper sent letters from those towns."

—◆—

The ticket office of the Long Island Railroad station on Atlantic Avenue was closed Christmas Eve, but a sign said the waiting room would be open Christmas Day. He rushed to the station just after dawn and was there when the doors were unlocked.

He found route maps in a wooden rack by the ticket booth and moved to the window for better light.

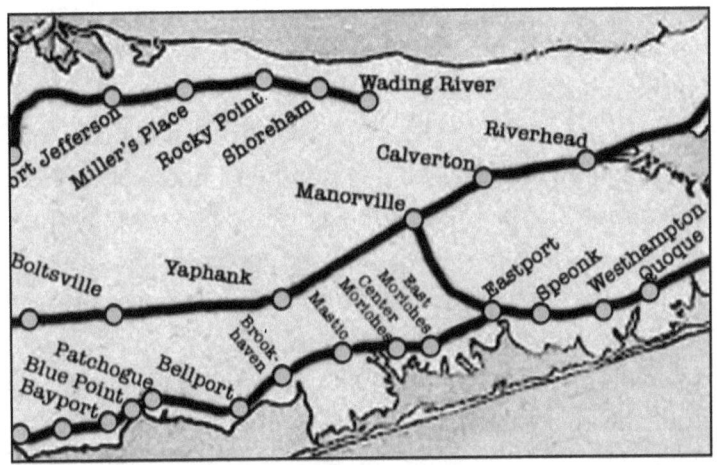

Railroad routes on Long Island

It was suddenly clear to him.

He rushed back to Clinton Avenue and to Sheenagh. Showing her the map, he explained the reasoning.

"The kidnapper sent all the letters from towns on the rail lines, eight of them. And they're all on either the central or southern routes, which you can reach by this connecting line from Eastport, here, to Manorville. What this says to me is that this man didn't have a motor himself, so that was how he'd reach those post offices. The train. And that's how he got to Hempstead in toward the city to steal a motor out of the station parking lot. The train."

"And you said he probably didn't send a letter from his own town, so he must live —"

"Near one of the other train stations on the central or southern line," Nolan said. "But which one?"

Just after eight the following morning, Sunday, with the deadline the kidnapper had given Hughes just a day away, Nolan boarded a train at Pennsylvania Station bound for Riverhead at the eastern end of Long Island on the railroad's central line.

The chances were the kidnapper lived along the central line, he had decided. The man had not expected his stolen motor to be linked to this case, so he probably traveled on the line on which he lived to reach Hempstead, as that was the easiest thing to do. And Hempstead was on the central line close to the city.

Nolan had also decided that Calverton and Riverhead were the two most likely towns in which the kidnapper lived. He had not sent letters from either. However, Riverhead was the county seat and considerably larger, so he decided to start there.

Few people rode the train east at that time of day, so Nolan found a seat in a parlor car close to a heater and as far as possible from the drafty doors. The city soon gave way to towns that gave way to villages. The landscape – barren, flat, and snow-covered – was monotonous enough that he could briefly fall asleep until the conductor's call of the next station would roughly wake him.

Three hours later, he stepped onto the platform at Riverhead. The station master was at lunch, so Nolan went in search of someone on Main Street to ask for information. As he passed the town clerk's office on the icy sidewalk, he saw someone inside despite it being Sunday. He knocked and showed his badge through the door glass as the man approached.

The man unlocked it but only cracked it open an inch.

"We're closed."

"It's an emergency," Nolan said.

He explained the situation, and, reluctantly, the man let him in.

"I wonder if I can see any typed letters from residents you might have so I can compare them to the photograph of the death threat. Sir, the boy's life is in danger or I wouldn't bother you."

The clerk, well past sixty, still acted as if this were a great imposition. He mumbled something Nolan could not hear as he went to collect the letters from a file drawer.

"Just the typed letters, sir," Nolan said. "Not the hand-written ones."

"I heard you the first time. Matter what kind of typed letter?"

"No, sir. Any kind."

In a moment, be brought Nolan two handfuls of about thirty letters each. "Sounds pretty far-fetched, if you ask me, that someone in our town would be part of some kid-napping way off in New York City, but here you go."

Nolan had to shake his head. About half the letters were handwritten.

As the clerk read a newspaper, Nolan went through them one by one, holding each typed page up against the photograph.

"Sir, can I ask you. Have you seen anyone the last cou-ple of weeks, someone coming in to town regularly who usually isn't here that often?"

"Could be a lot of people."

Clearly, the clerk had no intention of helping him. "Sir, it would be someone matching the description I gave you? About fifty, hates pacifists, wants the war."

When the clerk did not immediately answer, Nolan looked up to see he had put down the paper and was apparently thinking about something.

"In fact, there may be someone," he said. He went to another desk and searched through a stack of files. "Amos Woodhull. He's a duck-hunting guide. He lives by himself out in a cottage by the Peconic River."

"And he's been in town frequently the last two weeks?"

"Every day it seemed. I'd see him walk past here toward the train depot. I almost never see him in town." He was sifting through the file. "I remember Amos sent us a letter of complaint about his neighbors two months ago. He seems to think he's an inventor. I heard he's try-ing to sell a thing to the Navy, a balloon-type thing you blow up if you're in a lifeboat and the waves are about to swamp you. He says it would keep lifeboats afloat if there's a war and a ship gets torpedoed. One time I heard him say he blames the pacifists for why he can't sell it ... Here it is." He held up the letter. "He says his neighbors are too loud and it keeps him from getting the sleep he needs for his inventing work."

He handed it to Nolan then stood by as Nolan held it and the photograph side by side. The clerk, narrowing his eyes, leaned in.

"By God, that's it, ain't it!" the clerk fairly shouted.

Indeed, a perfect match. The d's and b's were all filled in, but the a's and o's were not. "This man Woodhull. Where does he live?"

The clerk wrote down directions. Excited by the idea he was part of a mission to capture a kidnapper, the clerk agreed to telephone the county sheriff as well as Baker and Keyes at the Brooklyn Detective Bureau while Nolan went straightaway to Woodhull's house.

⚜

Webber's Road ran along the Peconic River, which flowed east into Flander's Bay, which eventually emptied into Long Island Sound. On one end of the road were the estate-like summer cottages of the wealthy, who traveled out from New York City for the hot months. On the other end was a former Methodist summer camp, a collection of smaller, ramshackle cottages where some of the year-round residents lived. Nolan was told by the clerk that many were housekeepers, gardeners, and chauffeurs for the wealthy families. Woodhull's cottage ("The tan one with a canoe always leaning against the front of the house") was among them.

It had lightly snowed overnight. The day was sunny although bitterly cold. Nolan had to walk a quarter mile past the large cottages to find the camp, marked by a fading wooden sign posted on a tree. Camp Nathan Hale.

Woodhull's cottage

Immediately, he saw Woodhull's cottage with the canoe out front.

As if out only for a bracing walk in the winter sun, he strolled past it, glancing over quickly to see what he could make of the house. Two floors. Maybe six or seven rooms. In the driveway, amidst the snow, were recent tire tracks. What appeared to be a barn was in the back yard, and the river was apparently past the trees behind the barn.

At the end of the road, Nolan found a path down to the river, then he doubled back to the cottage, keeping low along the frozen riverbank. Coming up from the river, he looked into the rear window of the barn. Under a huge canvas sheet he could make out the shape of an automobile. Was it the stolen Ford? Then he saw the sheet did not fully hide the license tag. He moved to another window and rubbed away a glaze of ice. The three numbers he saw matched.

He studied the back of the cottage. There was a basement with a hatchway entrance. Darting from the side of the barn to the foundation of the cottage, he dropped to the snowy ground. Then, with as little noise as possible, he tried to slowly open the hatchway door. It lifted only an inch before a simple latch on the inside caught it. However, using a twig inserted into the gap, Nolan was able to lift the latch so the door could open.

The basement, with its uneven dirt floor, had firewood in several large piles. A couple of steamer trunks, some plumbing debris, and a tool bench took up much of the rest. There was a wooden staircase in the middle leading up to a room in the back of the house. Could it be the kitchen?

He stood very still. He could hear nothing upstairs. Quietly mounting the steps, he got to a height where he could lay on the stairs and see beneath the door. Indeed, it was the kitchen. The gap was large enough that he could make out the sink, an icebox, a kitchen table, and a firewood box. He could also see the stocks of two guns leaned against the far wall − a double-barreled shotgun, of the kind used for stalking birds, and a hunting rifle. He knew enough about hunting rifles to know this one was for considerably larger game than one would ever find on Long Island.

He guessed that the house was set up this way − the parlor in front, a dining room after that, then the kitchen in back.

Still hearing nothing in the house, he reached up and slowly turned the knob, then lightly pushed at the door. It was locked from the kitchen side. As he began to back down the stairs to find something among the tools to pry it open, he heard distant footsteps elsewhere in the house, perhaps on the second floor.

Nevertheless, he went to find a tool and located a large chisel. Now the footsteps were directly above him in the kitchen. Fearing they were headed to the basement, he hid behind a firewood stack. Quickly, he checked the safety latch on his revolver and felt his trouser pocket to make sure the handkerchief holding six additional bullets was still there.

Then he heard shouting, but not clearly enough to tell what was being said. He moved back to the stairs, the chisel in one hand, the revolver in the other, and could hear the voice, apparently Woodhull's.

"You don't have no right!"

A response came from outside somewhere, but it was not loud enough to understand. Nolan was sure it was the sheriff.

"Show me some law that says I have to!" Woodhull shouted. "This is a man's castle!"

There was another inaudible response from outside.

"Don't try!" Woodhull shouted. "Get off my property! No one gets in a man's castle!"

There was silence for a moment, then Woodhull came into the kitchen and picked up the shotgun. Nolan could see a box of shells on the kitchen table and, as Woodhull loaded, one shell fell to the floor. When he bent over enough to retrieve it, Nolan could see his face. Unshaven, about fifty, brown hair.

Picking up the rifle also, Woodhull rushed back to the parlor. A few second later, Nolan heard glass break. A window pane? Woodhull giving himself a place to shoot from? Then there was a shotgun blast followed by several shots from outside that sounded like pistol shots. More shouting followed.

Nolan tried to pry open the door with the chisel, working it only when he heard Woodhull shouting. The lock finally popped. Nolan pushed open the door and moved behind the firewood box, his heart pounding.

Should he just shoot the man? It made sense. The sheriff was under fire outside and the boy was likely upstairs. Innocent lives would be saved.

There were two entrances to the kitchen, a door from the dining room and a side door to a hallway and the second-floor staircase. Staying low, Nolan crept across the kitchen floor toward the hallway, but suddenly Woodhull, with his shotgun in hand, came back for his box of shells on the table. Seeing Nolan, he fired wildly as he was raising the shotgun. Nolan fired as well. The blast of birdshot from Woodhull slammed into the icebox then seemed to scatter everywhere in the kitchen, even shattering the window above the sink. Woodhull was screaming curses as he disappeared into the front room and Nolan could see blood on the floor where he had been standing, evidence his shot found its mark. Nolan examined himself. He saw a trickle of blood on his shoe and a stain near his calf, but felt little pain, only a dull ache.

"Woodhull! Give up!" he shouted.

Then there was a different sounding blast. The hunting rifle. The bullet tore through the kitchen wall from a front room and lodged in the opposite wall by the sink.

"Anyone tries to get at me, by God, you'll be dead and the boy'll be dead! I can shoot right through the ceiling and get him at any time! I know just where he's tied up!"

Just to let Woodhull know he was still there, Nolan fired a shot through the kitchen door toward the parlor. Then he heard shouting from outside again, several different voices, imploring Woodhull to give up.

Woodhull fired at the men outside. "Stay away!" he shouted, but his voice was strained and plaintive. How badly had he wounded Woodhull?

Nolan took a deep breath. He moved across the kitchen to the hallway and the stairwell. Leaning forward as far as he felt safe, he could not see Woodhull. He knew it was a poor calculation, but he looked back at where the rifle bullet entered the kitchen and where it hit on the opposite wall and figured the straight line out to the front room. It appeared he could cross the hallway without

being seen, but did he want to risk his life on that compu-
tation?

Suddenly, there was a volley of shots from outside,
breaking windows in the front of the house. Woodhull
sent a shotgun blast back at them, and as he did, Nolan
rushed to the stairwell, pressed against the wall, and
climbed the stairs.

He opened the first door he came to and Tom was
lying on a makeshift mattress of quilts on the floor,
gagged and tied up with cotton rope. Nolan did not undo
either. He quickly hoisted the stunned boy on his shoulder and carried him out into the hallway. With shooting
and shouting going on downstairs and outside, Nolan
went into the second bedroom at the back of the house,
Woodhull's bedroom, and dropped Tom on the bed. At
least if Woodhull fired into the ceiling of this room, the
mattress might slow or even stop the bullet.

Nolan looked out the back window. He could see a man
by the barn, apparently a sheriff's deputy, his revolver
drawn. He opened the window and waved several times at
him, hoping it would be correctly interpreted. When the
man did not fire, and instead waved back, Nolan removed
the ropes and gag from Tom.

"I'm going to drop you to the ground. There's snow
down there, so it won't be so bad. Can you run away from
the house when I do? There'll be a deputy waiting for you
by the barn."

"I think so."

However, when Nolan looked out the window again,
the deputy had crept up and was standing directly below.

"I'll lower the boy out," Nolan whispered. "I'm a private detective."

The deputy nodded.

The shooting downstairs halted momentarily and Woodhull turned to shouting nonstop in the front room. The damned pacifists, the damned police, the damned this, the damned that. So Nolan felt safe lowering the boy. With Tom's shoes dangling six or seven feet above the ground, Nolan dropped him into the deputy's arms. Then they both rushed through the snow to the safety of the barn.

In a moment, Nolan heard a commotion in the kitchen below. Then the rifle fired, sending a bullet into the front room where Tom had been. Nolan got onto the bed. There was another shot from beneath him and a bullet ripped through the duck-feather mattress two feet in front of where Nolan was huddled.

Then he heard steps on the stairs.

"Any room you and the boy are in, I'll get one of you!"

Then the steps were in the hallway and there was another shot. A bullet flew through the wall, hitting six feet from Nolan's head. He heard Woodhull reloading and knew he had to make a decision. Mustering his courage and with his revolver in hand, he jumped from the bed and dove sideways into the hallway, getting off two shots as he hit the floor. Woodhull fired simultaneously with the hunting rifle, but, expecting an upright target, he had been aiming high and missed. Nolan's shots hit the mark, though.

Woodhull fell back, grabbing at his neck. When he started to raise the rifle again, Nolan fired twice more at his right arm. That was enough. Screaming in pain, Woodhull dropped the rifle and Nolan jumped up off the floor and kicked it away. Blood was streaming from

Woodhull's neck and arm, so Nolan took out his handkerchief, keeping the bullets.

"Press it against your neck," he said. "If you stay still, we'll get you a doctor."

Nolan cupped his hands and shouted toward the front of the house, "The kidnapper is shot! This is detective John Nolan and he's badly wounded but the boy is safe! I handed him down to one of your agents in the back yard!"

"We hear you! We've got the boy! We're coming in! Don't shoot!"

"You don't shoot either!"

One of the first people up the stairs after the sheriff was the town clerk. "I called your friend Baker and he and the boy's father are driving out. He said to tell you Keyes had to go into the hospital to pass a kidney stone."

That made Nolan laugh, as much from the humor of it as the relief he felt.

As the sheriff examined Woodhull, the hallway quickly filled with neighbors and others who had heard the shooting, taking on the air of a raucous men's smoker. Mistaken for one of the late arrivals, Nolan was able to slip down the stairs to the kitchen where he got a clean rag to bandage his calf. It appeared the buckshot only grazed him.

Outside, he found Tom wrapped in a blanket in the back seat of a police motor in the street.

"You all right? Did the police give you anything to eat?"

"Not yet. I'm all right, I guess."

"I'll get you some food. I saw bread in the kitchen. Did Woodhull feed you?"

"Was that his name? He fed me fish and potatoes and that was all. But he let me drink beer a few times. My father never let me drink beer. I heard you shot Woodhull."

"I did."

"With your Smith and Wesson? Maybe I'll get a Smith and Wesson after all ... Thanks for what you did, sir."

They both smiled warmly at each other.

"I'll be back," Nolan said.

He started to the house. Trudging across the yard, the snow trampled down by dozens of footprints, he wondered what American boys liked to eat. Then he thought of Sheenagh and wondered what his own child would be, a boy or girl. If it was a boy, growing up in Brooklyn, it would be an American boy, he realized, with American tastes.

He stopped a moment when he reached the front porch, suddenly exhausted, in need of food himself. With the excitement subsiding, it occurred to him all that had happened in the last fifteen minutes.

He leaned against a railing, shaking, and as he waited for his strength to return, he found himself idly running names for a baby boy through his thoughts.

THE END

Fortunato Ricci

Celeste Galienda

Mrs. Taylor

Miss Henshaw

Mrs. Granados

MURDER AT THE MET

"The stolen instrument – you called it a what?" John Nolan asked.

"An Amati. It's a type of violin."

They sat in the living room of Nolan's apartment on Clinton Avenue in Brooklyn. It was a Tuesday in late March of 1918 and the cold winter, made more harsh by news of Allied losses in the European war, was finally giving way to warmer weather.

A private detective, Nolan had no office. However, clients seemed to like the informality of his apartment, with his wife Sheenagh serving coffee and his two-year-old daughter shyly popping in and out of the room. Indeed, he had no shortage of business. His advertisement ran four times a month in the *Brooklyn Daily Eagle*. That and recommendations from former clients as an honest and able detective would regularly bring new clients to his door.

"Mr. Ricci," Nolan said. "I apologize for my ignorance of your profession. I grew up in a small village in Ireland."

"Please don't apologize," Ricci said. "I'm sure I'm just as ignorant of your profession. I grew up in a small village in Italy."

"How did you go from that simple life to the Metropolitan Opera?"

Ricci told of being a child prodigy, of being supported in his musical training by a wealthy sponsor, and of being, for two decades, a violinist in orchestras across Europe before coming to America and gaining a position at the Metropolitan in 1913.

As Ricci spoke, Nolan could barely hear his Italian heritage in his accent. Apparently, working in so many other European countries for so long had overwhelmed it.

Nolan saw the same thing beginning to happen to his own accent after only four years in America. He wondered if, in a few more years, the American English he heard around him daily would finally smother what remained of Ireland in his voice.

As he listened, Nolan took notes in a leather pocket diary and also studied Ricci. Appearing to be in his late forties, he was a heavy man but elegantly dressed in a swallowtail coat, his long hair slicked straight back. He was shy, warm-hearted (each time his daughter entered the room, Ricci would make an astonished face that delighted Erin) – and he was deeply distraught over the loss of his violin.

"And your Amati, your violin. When was it stolen?"

"Three days ago," he said.

Ricci said the instrument was taken from his residence in Brooklyn Heights late on the afternoon of March twenty-third while he was getting a steam at the Brooklyn Sporting Club. The violin was in its case and the case was wrapped in soft cloth and kept in the laundry hamper in his bathroom, beneath soiled clothes. The front door of the apartment was forced open, apparently with a crowbar, but nothing else in the apartment was disturbed or stolen.

"If I don't get my Amati back, it would be the worst thing that ever happened to me. I loved that violin. I can't replace it."

"Perhaps you should know, Mr. Ricci, my fee is —"

"Please, it's just Ricci. My full name is Fortunato Ricci, but everyone has always called me just Ricci."

"Ricci. My fee is eight dollars a day plus expenses. What if it takes me ten days to find your Amati violin, assuming I can? That would be more than eighty dollars. Wouldn't it make more sense for you to just buy a new Amati violin and hope you can come to love your new violin as much?"

Ricci smiled. "My Amati is worth more than five thousand dollars. That's why I can't replace it."

"Are you joking?"

"You've heard of Stradivarius violins? Stradivari was an apprentice of Nicolò Amati and in my opinion an Amati is second only to a Strad in the quality of its sound. What these instrument makers did, it's never been duplicated."

Sheenagh came in from the kitchen with a serving tray. "Mr. Ricci, I brought —"

"Please, it's just Ricci. My first name is Fortunato, but everyone just calls me Ricci."

"Ricci, here, help yourself."

"Sir," Sheenagh asked as she placed a sugar bowl on the tray. "I heard you mention you were a violinist. Who do you play for?"

Ricci took his cup of coffee. "I play for the Metropolitan Opera."

Sheenagh stood upright. "*The* Metropolitan Opera? Here in New York?"

"Yes. I'm part of the orchestra."

"Oh goodness! That's wonderful!" she said. "Are you going to be here for a few minutes more? There's some-one – if you don't mind – someone who would love to meet you."

Ricci beamed. "It would be a pleasure."

Sheenagh rushed out to the hallway.

"Sir, you mentioned you'd been trying to sell the instrument."

"Yes, through a dealer near Union Square over in Manhattan. But I refused to let it out of my sight. If he had someone who wanted to see it, they had to come to me in Brooklyn."

"How many people came to see the violin?"

"Only three."

"Did they see you remove it from where you'd hidden it?"

"I would make them wait in my parlor while I got it, and I would close the door to the parlor as I went to the bathroom to take it out. So I don't believe they knew where it was."

However, the fact the apartment was otherwise undis-turbed by the thief told Nolan someone knew exactly where it was.

"Another question. Without your violin, how do you still play?"

"The Metropolitan will lend me a violin, but just for their performances."

"And why were you trying to sell this instrument if you loved it so much?"

Ricci shifted uneasily on the sofa. "I need the money for a personal reason."

"What reason, if you don't mind my asking?"

"There's a financial opportunity, a stock in a mining company that's become available. It's quite a rare opportunity."

Nolan looked up from his notes. "Mr. Ricci ... Ricci ... Who's trying to sell you this stock?"

The story Ricci told, from its beginning, struck Nolan as a classic of its kind – a pure investing swindle. Although he had just turned thirty and had only emigrated from Ireland in early 1914, Nolan had experienced enough of life in New York City to know fraud when he saw it.

Ricci told him that having a thousand dollars of savings to invest, he visited the office of a broker in Manhattan. After talking to the broker a few minutes, a man rushed in and interrupted. The man, who was a client of the broker, said his cousin, who was an engineer for a copper mining company in Arizona, wired him that morning that an unusually rich vein of ore had just been discovered. The find had not been made public yet, but when it was, the privately held stock was going to soar in price.

The rest of the story involved Ricci offering to join the man and the broker in a purchase of a large block of the stock and a midnight meeting at the Hotel Belleclaire on Broadway with the ex-wife of the company's founder who held the stock.

"I need to sell the violin to raise additional funds for this purchase. It could make me rich."

Nolan put down his pen. "Ricci, first, under no conditions should you be part of this stock purchase. I guarantee you, it's a swindle. Let me look into it for you."

"Oh, no. Please. I know this is real. I did research. I went to the library. This company exists and they have mines in Arizona and Nevada. And I found an article in the *Times* last Friday saying they opened a new mine in Jerome, Arizona, just three months ago. And that's where this discovery was made."

"These swindlers do their research too, sir. I'm sure they saw that same article. They try to make these offers sound as real as possible. Please, let me call some people and ask some questions. Wait before you do anything. Let's see what I can find."

"You'll find what I found, which is that this is a real opportunity. But I welcome any additional information you can gather. So, yes, I'll wait. They've given me another week to get more funds. The find won't be made public until at least then."

"One other question. I imagine you're paid well by the Metropolitan Opera. Why do you need money from this stock investment so badly that you would consider selling your violin?"

Ricci sighed heavily. "It's about love. That's all I'm going to say. It's about a singer with the Metropolitan."

Nolan heard a commotion in the front hallway and, in a moment, Sheenagh was in the door with their upstairs neighbor, Benjamin Shapiro, who had a violin under his arm.

Shapiro did not wait to be introduced. "Sir. It's just such a pleasure to meet you. I'm no professional violinist. My violin's cheap and any music I make from it is poor. So I was wondering if you could play a few bars of something so that I and this cheap violin could understand what real music is."

Ricci sprang from the sofa, smiling broadly. Apparently nothing appealed to him so much as the chance to perform.

"I would love to."

Now others from the building were crowding into the hall. More Shapiros, Mrs. Giretti, the Beys, Mrs. McCormick. Several children (from what families Nolan was not sure) pushed to the front row.

Ricci waved them all in, backing up to give them proper room, before he took a seat to play.

"This is Tartini's 'Devil's Trill' sonata. May you enjoy it."

<hr>

Ricci gave Nolan the business card of his broker, Foster Brothers Investments. At eight o'clock Wednesday morning, Nolan exited the subway and walked up Broadway toward the Park Row Building in the financial district.

A group of Navy seamen approached him on the sidewalk. Although the war was in Europe, its evidence was seen throughout the city. Ships of all kinds, from troop transports to Naval destroyers, constantly arrived at and left from the New York piers. And while their ships were in port, soldiers and seamen wandered the streets at all times of day and night looking for food, drink, women, and entertainment.

As he passed, Nolan admired the Navy men's dress uniforms, the white jumpers and trousers trimmed in blue, but he knew it was unlikely he would ever wear one. He was thirty but still a year away from being able to apply for United States citizenship. Nevertheless, he received a draft notice in July of 1917, several months after America entered the war. He reported to his district's exemption board on a Saturday morning at Erasmus Hall High School in Brooklyn. Knowing he would be exempted both as a resident alien and as the sole support of his wife and child, he did not tell Sheenagh until the following day. She would only have worried.

At twenty-nine stories, the Park Row building had been the tallest commercial building in the world a decade earlier. Now more than a dozen buildings in lower Manhattan surpassed it in height.

The Park Row Building

Inside, it was a rabbit warren of tiny offices – it contained nearly a thousand – and it took Nolan twenty minutues to locate the broker's office on the eighteenth floor. While the brokerage's name was on the door, the door was locked and, peering through the glass, the office looked empty of furnishings.

Nolan went to the office across the hall. Wm. Coolidge III, Certified Public Accountant. The door was open and a man in a business suit was just hanging up his coat and rolling up his shirtsleeves.

"I'm looking for Louis W. Foster, the broker. Do you know if he's going to be in today?"

"Don't know, friend. Got work to do," he said, closing the door.

There was always a moment when Nolan first spoke to someone. A question would hang in the air. You can hear by my accent I'm Irish. What's your reaction to that? The person's expression and tone of voice would instantly provide the answer.

With this man, the answer was quite clear. Move along, Paddy.

Manhattan was a collection of tiny countries packed onto a tiny island, and although only streets and avenues created the borders between them, it was as if these nations were separated by great walls and armed barricades.

In the densely packed lower east side of Manhattan, nearly half the residents of the various assembly districts were foreign-born, mainly Irish, Germans, Italians, and European Jews, but there were also enclaves of Hungarians, Greeks, and Chinese. And they all had their neighborhoods.

For instance, the Germans lived from 1st to 8th Street and the Jewish quarter extended from Houston to Monroe Street. Hostility, insults, and slurs often greeted the immigrants who ventured beyond the confines of their neighborhood. And for the Irish, one of the first immigrant groups to arrive in the city, the prejudice against them was widespread.

Nolan waited outside the Foster Brothers' door for a more friendly office occupant to appear on the hallway, and one soon did, a man searching his pockets for the key to unlock the door next to the Fosters'.

"Sir, I was looking for the Foster Brothers."

"You might be looking all day," the man said, "They moved to another address Wednesday afternoon. But I can recommend another broker if you're looking for one, which is myself."

"No thanks. Do you know where the Fosters' office is now?"

"Are you a postal inspector?"

"I'm not."

"Manhattan police?"

"No."

"You might try the seventh floor downstairs. But if you are the police, don't tell them who sent you."

Nolan had to go to the building manager's office on the first floor to find where on the seventh floor Foster Brothers had relocated. Asked why they had moved, the manager shook his head. "They never tell me. They've moved three times in a year."

Nolan prepared his story on the way up in the elevator. He would say he was looking for a fictitious investment company. The Fosters would likely offer their services. He knocked on the open door of seven thirty-six.

"Excuse me. I'm looking for Manheim Investments. It's a brokerage recommended to me. Do you know if they're on this floor?"

Two men who looked like twins turned – forty, balding

in identical ways, putting on weight around their middle in identical ways.

"Manheim? I heard he's in South America for the spring. But if you're looking for a broker, you've found two of the best." One came forward and extended his hand. "Louis W. Foster. This is my brother Fred. We're the Foster Brothers. We have our main office uptown near Central Park but we wanted to have a presence downtown also, so we're just opening up here. Why don't you come in."

Nolan said he had recently inherited a thousand dollars. "I've read so much about people turning small sums into large sums in the stock market that I wanted to try that, but my problem is I know so little about investing."

"Well, you've stumbled onto the two of the most knowledgeable men about stocks in New York to guide you. We've got more than thirty years of experience between us."

Fred excused himself, saying he needed to go across the street to the bank.

Louis, who seemed to be the brother in charge, told Nolan to sit, dusting off a chair for him, then asked him questions about himself.

Nolan's responses were these: born in Ireland, a railroad worker, single, a tenement apartment on 101st Street.

It took only ten minutes for the swindle to start. Nolan had to hold a laugh when it did, as the details were so similar to Ricci's experience.

A man, not Fred but similar in appearance (a third brother perhaps), rushed in and breathlessly spilled his story.

Louis interrupted. "Mr. Coleman, please, get your breath. You say your cousin works for what mining company?"

More of the story. The copper strike in Jerome, Arizona. The certainty the stock would soar when it became public.

"This is not a public stock, though. It's privately held," Coleman said. "But I know someone who has a large block and is willing to sell some of it. She doesn't know a thing about the strike this morning. So we have to move quickly."

"How much does she want?"

"Five thousand for what she wants to sell. But I only have three thousand. What about you Louis?"

"My money isn't liquid at the moment. It's all tied up in options. I only have about a thousand I could get today."

A silence followed and again Nolan had to hold his laughter. It was like sitting in the front row of a burlesque show.

Foster looked at Nolan. "By any chance, is this something —"

"That I might want to get in on? Maybe. Who holds this block of stock?"

"The ex-wife of the company's founder," Coleman said. "She lives at the Belleclaire Hotel on lower Broadway. She's a rich woman already, so I don't mind in the least taking her money. In her mind, she's taking ours. I'm sure she thinks it's worthless stock."

"Let me ask you," Nolan said. "I have a friend who's got some funds saved, about a thousand dollars. Would you let a fourth person be part of this? "

"Indeed we would," Foster said, the "we" all but admitting his conspiracy in the swindle.

"The only thing is my friend and I would need to meet the ex-wife, to make sure this is legitimate, before we hand over our funds."

"I'd expect nothing less," Foster said. "Mr. Coleman, can you set up a meeting for this evening, say around eight o'clock? We'll meet in the lobby of the Belleclaire by the bell captain's station."

＊

Nolan and Jack Baker, a Brooklyn police detective he had worked with several times, were waiting in the lobby of the Belleclaire. It was already ten minutes past eight, but neither the Foster brothers nor Coleman had appeared.

"They smelled something," Baker said. "My guess is you'll find they cleared out of their new office also."

"Why do you think more people haven't reported being swindled by these men?"

"Simple. They never knew they were. They handed over their money thinking they just bought the stock and a week later they got a call. 'The ore wasn't worth much after all,' the broker would tell them. 'It's contaminated. Now the stock price is crashing. You might want to sell quick so you get some of your money back.' Then they'd get a check in the mail the next week from the broker. Seventy cents on the dollar. 'Oh well,' they think. 'Just a bad investment.' But they're happy to get anything back at all."

＊

In fact, the brokers' office in the Park Row Building was empty the following morning. Nolan wanted to kick himself. He was sure it was his story about looking for

Manheim Investments. It was likely the Fosters had run into the broker from the eighteenth floor who had sent Nolan down to the seventh. Nolan imagined what this other broker told them. "He said he was looking for you, not someone named Manheim. Must have been the police after all."

—◈—

"Where will you be?" Sheenagh asked as she spoon-fed their daughter her farina.

"In Manhattan most of the morning." Nolan said, gulping the last of his coffee. "I'm going to visit the violin broker who sent three people to see Ricci's violin."

Their parlor telephone rang. Nolan rose from the kitchen table to answer it. "Then, hopefully, I'll be home for lunch."

He grabbed the phone before the second bell sounded. "Nolan Detective Bureau."

"This is James McCann, a guard over at the Tombs."

"Sure Jimmy, I remember you."

"You have a client what got arrested late last night who's in here, and he's asking for you."

"What's his name?"

"Ricci. Something Ricci."

"Arrested for what?"

"Murder."

—◈—

Nolan made a series of calls that began with the Classon Avenue precinct in Brooklyn. Then the calls moved over to Manhattan and eventually to the city's First Branch Detective Bureau where he finally got answers from a detective he knew on the force.

A performer, another violinist for the Metropolitan

Opera, was shot to death in an upstairs hallway of the opera house not long after Ricci and the man were seen arguing by several people. Apparently, the two argued frequently. And Mr. Ricci had recently purchased a double-barrel pocket pistol, believed to be the kind of small weapon that killed the man, although the pistol was not found at the scene or on Ricci.

"Did anyone witness the shooting?"

"I'm just looking at the arrest report here," the detective said, "and I don't see nothing like that. Looks circumstantial so far, but that'll change quick. It's the Metropolitan Opera, so it'll be a big story and everyone'll want to get their name in the papers. The district attorney's already been over asking about it, so's it's gonna be a circus. I already feel sorry for your man."

Hearing the news and hearing that Nolan planned to go talk to Ricci, Sheenagh demanded to go with him. Their upstairs neighbors agreed to watch Erin, so they took the elevated train over to Manhattan in the early afternoon.

The Tombs was the massive city prison in lower Manhattan that sat across the street from the Criminal Courts Building. The two were connected by an enclosed walkway called the "Bridge of Sighs" that crossed four stories above the street between them. Nolan heard it got that name because as prisoners were led from the court to the prison, they would sigh as they got their last look at freedom below.

At the prison, Nolan and Sheenagh were taken to the visitors' room and told Ricci would be brought in. The room had long oak tables that were scrubbed every morning with a strong disinfectant that could still be

The "Bridge of Sighs" connecting the Tombs prison, left, with the Criminal Courts Building

smelled this late in the day.

Ricci, in wrist shackles, was soon brought in. His eyes were red and his face was drained of color. Sheenagh began to reach across the table to touch his arm, but a guard lightly tapped her shoulder with his nightstick to stop her. She pulled the hand back.

"Ricci. What happened?" Nolan asked.

"I don't know."

"You don't know anything?"

"No one's told me anything except that Granados was shot to death. It was not me. John, Sheenagh, I didn't do this and it's a nightmare, an utter nightmare, what's happened to me."

"Who is Granados?" Nolan asked.

"He was our first seat. Our first violinist. Alfredo Granados."

"Do you have a lawyer?"

"A man the court made me use for the arraignment. But what's a lawyer for if you didn't do anything?"

"We'll find someone else. But tell me everything that happened."

His mouth trembling at times, Ricci related the story of his last twenty hours. At seven o'clock the previous evening, they were readying for a benefit performance of *Rigoletto*. Enrico Caruso was to sing the role of Il Duca. The revenue was to go to the Fund for Italian War Widows. The front doors had been opened to patrons and Ricci had just taken his seat in the orchestra. Two men were brought to the orchestra pit by the stage manager, who pointed at Ricci. Then one of the men whispered in his ear, "You've got to come with us."

"I said 'has someone died' and they both looked at each other and smiled. But I thought a relative had died and they were about to inform me who. They took me upstairs to the dressing area and had me look at the body lying in the hallway. There was a bloody bullet hole where Granados' eye had been. They made me stare at it, with a dozen other policemen standing around, just studying me. I was shaking at what was happening."

Ricci said he was taken to the Criminal Courts Building, arraigned, then transferred to the Tombs.

"In the court, the lawyer from the district attorney's office said I'm an Italian national and shouldn't be bonded, that I'm being charged with first-degree murder.

Everything he said to the judge, he would then turn around and repeat it slowly for the newspaper reporters in the first row behind him. He kept calling me the Italian national in a particularly ugly manner. When he did, they all would sneer at me, even this lawyer. A nightmare."

"This pistol – did you own one?"

"A derringer? Yes. Several of our musicians and performers bought them too. We've had some robberies of people who would leave alone late after a show, so a salesman from Remington came in and sold them to us and showed us how to use them. I ride the trains home to Brooklyn late at night and wanted one."

"Where is the pistol now? Do police have it?"

"It's in the violin case that was stolen. I kept it in the bag I had sewn into it for storage of the leather straps. But I've never fired it once, not once."

"Ricci, did you argue with the victim?"

He swallowed with difficulty, as if his mouth were severely parched. "Yes, I did. But so what? Everyone disliked this man. Others argued with him too. He was Spanish and he would not leave women in the company alone even though he was married. It was appalling."

"But did you argue with him just before he was shot?"

"I don't know what time he was shot. I —"

"Ricci, be honest. Did you argue with him earlier yesterday afternoon?"

"I ... I suppose I did."

Sheenagh, who had been silent, leaned forward. "Ricci, you told John there was a woman, a singer with the Metropolitan, who you had feelings for. Does this involve her?"

Ricci sighed heavily. "Yes."

"Was the argument yesterday about her?" she asked.

Ricci nodded reluctantly. "But John, Sheenagh, please." His eyes were tearing. "I did not shoot this man. Let God be my witness. I did not."

"Tell us about this woman, if you would," Sheenagh said. Without thinking, she reached to touch Ricci's hand but the guard rapped the table with his nightstick.

"This visit's over. Prisoner, let's go."

After putting Sheenagh on the elevated back to Brooklyn, Nolan went by the First Branch Detective Bureau in Manhattan and was able to view the evidence photos and read the detectives' reports.

There was a publicity photo of Granados from the Metropolitan Opera Company as well as several photos of the murder scene and statements of those who had

Police evidence photos

witnessed the two men arguing.

As Nolan left the building, Jack Baker stopped him at the door.

"You better be prepared. The DA, Swann — he's already tipped his hand. Another Italian murdering someone. Let's make an example of this one, he'll tell the jury."

❖

RENOWNED VIOLINIST MOURNED TODAY

Another violinist held as chief suspect in his murder with jealousy the apparent motive

District Attorney Swann vows swift and sure prosecution

Alfredo Granados, the internationally celebrated violinist, will be mourned this afternoon in a ceremony at four o'clock at the Metropolitan Opera House.

Meanwhile, Fortunato Ricci, the suspected killer, occupies a cell at the Tombs prison awaiting a true bill from the Grand Jury and eventual trial.

Mr. Granados has been the first violin for the opera company's orchestra for most of the last year as a visiting artist. Mr. Ricci was the third violin. Mr. Granados was shot to death outside the performers' dressing rooms in the opera house on W. 39th Street Thursday evening.

"Our Metropolitan Opera is beloved by New Yorkers and such a brazen murder is like the murder of a family member," said the district attorney, Edward Swann. "I will not stop until punishment has been exacted."

Swann said Mr. Ricci is an Italian national who was apparently upset at the attention Mr. Granados was paying to a singer whom Mr. Ricci had been pursuing romantically. Also, Mr. Granados had complained to the manager of the company that Mr. Ricci was an inferior violinist in the matter of playing certain pieces, something Mr. Ricci heard about and resented.

"So it appears both romantic and professional jealousy are the motives," Mr. Swann said.

Mr. Ricci's small pistol, believed to be the murder weapon, has not been recovered, but the pea-sized bullet taken from Mr. Granados' body match-

**es what a derringer of the type
Mr. Ricci owned would fire.**

**In addition, Mr. Ricci was seen
by two members of the opera
company arguing with Mr.
Granados just prior to the shooting.**

**Mr. Granados, who was 48
years old, was a native of Madrid,
Spain. He leaves his former wife,
Isabelle Granados, and one child
by her, both of whom live in
Madrid. He also leaves his current wife in New York City, the
former Ethel Swados, who served
for several years as his personal
secretary.**

Nolan was told he could not return to visit Ricci until
the following Monday. In the meantime, he had to find
the Amati if that was where the derringer was indeed
hidden.

In his first visit to Nolan's Brooklyn apartment, Ricci
had given Nolan a description of his stolen instrument.
While Amatis tended to look the same, he said, his had a
feature that would quickly identify it – a fault in the label
inside the instrument, visible through one of the "f"
holes, the facing holes on the front of the violin, to each
side of the strings, that helped project the sound. The
words on the label, which Ricci wrote down for him,
were, "Nicolaus Amatus Cremonae Hieronymus et
Antonius Nepos fecit anno 1664." However, on its right
side, the label was obscured by a poorly applied layer of

lacquer, so that one could barely read the words "fecit anno 1664."

The dealer who had sent Ricci potential buyers was located on Fifth Avenue near Union Square, a short trolley ride uptown from the Park Row Building.

Nolan had two theories. The first was that the dealer was behind the theft, that one of the buyers he sent to Ricci was there to determine the hiding place, which was passed on to the dealer. The second theory was that one of the buyers was the thief and that the dealer had nothing to do with it.

If the dealer was the thief, it was unlikely he had the stolen instrument in his shop – but it was not impossible. Just a month earlier, a philatelist stole the extremely rare signature of Button Gwinnett, one of the fifty-six signers of the Declaration of Independence, from a collector in the city who had assembled the full set of signatures through the purchase of letters and legal papers signed by the men. The philatelist, who had a shop selling rare stamps and documents, had gone to the collector's home for dinner. A day later, right in his own shop, the dealer tried to sell the stolen item to an undercover police detective for $2,800.

Ricci's dealer had his shop on the second floor above Branden's Furs on Fifth Avenue, with its own plate-glass window and sign looking over the street. "Home of Ward's Fine Musical Instruments." Because of the expense of the instruments he sold, one had to press a buzzer to be admitted. Nolan did so and in a moment an elderly man with a white beard came to the door, cracking it open an inch but keeping the chain in place.

"Can I help you?"

"Yes, sir. If you're the owner, I'm looking to buy a violin."

"So judging from your accent, you're Irish, are you. Are you a musician also? Our instruments are generally sold to professionals. These are expensive pieces."

"The man I represent has a son who wants to be a violinist. He would be buying this as a birthday present for the boy. He's interested in finding an Amati violin. He's under the impression that it's not as expensive as a Stradivarius, but it has nearly the same quality."

Still showing some suspicion, he let Nolan in. Every kind of instrument was displayed behind glass on the shelves, from clarinets and cornets to trumpets and trombones.

A younger man came from the back of the shop and stood silently in the doorway, arms folded, with just as much suspicion in his demeanor as the owner. He was Nolan's height but a good deal brawnier.

"This is my grandson. So tell me, what age is this young man with the birthday?"

"Fifteen. His father wants to buy him the finest Amati violin you have."

The owner eyed Nolan for a moment. "I have three right now that you might want to look at."

They were brought out by the grandson and placed on a counter atop a large piece of burlap.

The dealer gave a brief history of each. Nolan asked for a light to study them more closely, so an electric lamp was brought over. Peering in the pair of f-shaped holes in the waist of each instrument, he saw labels in each, but none that matched Ricci's description. However, doing this raised the owner's suspicions further.

Three Amati violins

"You're not a buyer for anyone, are you, Mick?" The owner said. "What's this about?"

"Mr. Ricci's violin. By now, you know it was stolen."

"I'm about to ask my grandson to come around and throw you out of here on your ear."

Nolan looked up and smiled at the young man who was glaring at him, apparently itching for the chance.

"He shouldn't try. I'm a private detective and I guarantee you I've been in a lot more fights than your grandson. I grew up fighting. It's his ear that would hit the floor. Not mine."

Nolan continued to smile and, releasing a single button, he let his jacket fall away from his chest to show his holstered revolver. The young man's smile faded.

"First, if I had Mr. Ricci's instrument," the owner said, "I wouldn't be showing it around."

"Maybe so, maybe not. You might want a quick sale to get rid of it and thought I would be it."

"I've made my reputation by being honest. I wouldn't jeopardize that for one violin."

"How is it you sent three buyers to look at his violin, and within days it's stolen by someone who knew exactly where it was? I'm guessing it was one of these buyers. If that gets into the newspapers, how does that affect your reputation? If you want this kept quiet, just give me the names of the buyers you sent."

Reluctantly, the owner complied.

⟨◇⟩

Monday morning, Nolan returned alone to the Tombs to see Ricci, who entered the room looking even more sad and miserable than during the first visit.

Worrying their time would be cut short, Nolan asked the difficult question first. "You have to tell me about this woman and this argument. Who is she?"

Ricci took a deep breath and glanced at the guard. His whisper to Nolan seemed gauged to keep their conversation between only them.

"First, let me tell you why I came to New York. My father, who began life quite poor, became a rich man in the sugar trade in northern Italy. When I was young and began to study violin, my mother presented me with the Amati. She believed that with such a violin in my hands I was destined to become famous. But this wasn't what happened. I played for many years in Germany, Italy, and England, but I was rarely a featured player and my mother was greatly disappointed.

So I came to America, in part, to escape my mother's poor opinion of me."

"But what about the woman and the argument?" Nolan asked.

"The woman I've spoken of, she's a contralto who sings in the chorus of our company. Mme. Galienda. Several times, she's been a featured singer for us. A fine voice. She's from the town of Soave, which is just five miles from my town of birth, Caldiero. But we didn't meet each other until New York. She's three years younger than me, and divorced, I've heard, after an unhappy marriage ... The problem I have is this. As with my mother, I don't measure up with her either. I'm only the third violin in our orchestra. At night, she leaves for late suppers with men whose names might be Astor or Rockefeller or Dodge. She would never leave with me."

"Ricci, women are strange creatures," Nolan said. "She might feel that, because she works with them, musicians are not for her. You say Astors and Rockefellers. Maybe she decided that rich men are —"

"Yes. Rich men. Don't you see? That's what she wants. She doesn't care that I'm a musician, just that I have little money. I need to be able to invite her to a fine restaurant night after night and not worry about the expense. A rich musician is still a rich man."

"But if you made a lot of money," Nolan said, "there'd be no guarantee —"

He put up his hand. "The guarantee is that if I don't have money, then she certainly won't be interested in me. So money is the first step."

"But there are so many other women in New York,

women who would give anything to go to dinner with a musician with the Metropolitan."

"John, there's a profound line from one of your American poets. 'The heart wants what it wants or else it does not care.' You and Sheenagh – how did you meet?"

"We met in grammar school in Ireland."

"So you fell in love early. That's wonderful. Did not your hearts want what they wanted? The evidence is right there in your home these many years later."

"What about the argument, though? What started it?"

Ricci's expression soured. "The argument, well, it wasn't an argument. I said some things to him but he didn't respond."

"What things?"

"Just … some things."

"Ricci, tell me exactly what you said."

"I called him … a … vile … nasty … detestable … bastard. Exactly those words."

Nolan shook his head. "And people heard this?"

"Several other people were in the hallway and I might have said it loudly. I was angry. He told the Met's manager I make mistakes when I played, which was not true. Absolutely not true."

"What about this contralto?"

"And he was bothering her, like he did to so many women. So I was mad about that too. Vile nasty detestable bastard. That's what I called him." Ricci broke into a smile. "Maybe those were the last words spoken to him. I can only hope so."

—◈—

As he left the prison, Nolan learned the board of directors of the Metropolitan Opera had engaged a defense attorney for Ricci. That afternoon, he went to see the lawyer in his office on West 41st Street to offer his services as an investigator in the case.

The ancient brick building, recently purchased, was being renovated floor by floor as tenants' leases expired and they vacated. The lawyer, on the top floor, had not yet left. On his door was a sign.

NATHAN de LEVAL
Duly qualified attorney
WILL DEFEND YOU
IF YOU ARE ACCUSED
Since 1886

The dusty office had just two rooms, the front one for his secretary, legal books, and a chair for clients who were waiting, and a smaller room in the rear for de Leval. Next to the client's chair hung a plaque.

A good lawyer knows the law.
A clever lawyer knows the judge.

The attorney, white-haired and spindly, said he was busy with other cases. "So I might hire you since you already know some things about the man. It'll cost me less. What experience do you have?"

Nolan only had to mention his association with three cases that had been in the news for de Leval to raise his hand. "Good enough. You're hired. But don't run up the bill, given the circumstances."

"What circumstances?"

"Well, the man looks very guilty, and this district attorney, Swann, is out to get him. The newspapers already have him convicted. This is not a case of innocent until proven guilty. It's a case of guilty until proven innocent. And it's my experience you don't waste too much time trying to do a thing that is impossible in a case like this, which is to make a man who is very likely guilty look innocent."

Nolan was astonished he would admit this. "But he truly might be innocent."

The attorney smiled. "You're a young man. When you're older —"

"No, I mean it. I believe he's innocent. There were other members of the company who also owned these derringers. And this man who was murdered – many people had grudges against him."

The attorney shrugged. His secretary was at the door indicating someone else was waiting.

"Well, you look into it, but stay out of Swann's way. I'm up against him on two other cases and I don't want to get on his bad side."

⟵◈⟶

At police headquarters, Nolan again read through the detectives' reports in the case. Four members of the company, including Ricci, purchased Remington Model 95 double derringers. Among them was Mme. Galienda, the woman Ricci had pursued. The other two buyers were members of the chorus, Mrs. Clara Taylor and Miss Fredericka Henshaw.

The reports said that all the pistols, except Ricci's, were examined the day after the murder and all had been recently fired.

The bullet had been recovered from the victim, but Nolan knew of no method to connect a particular bullet to any particular gun, other than saying the caliber of the two was the same.

According to the detectives' reports, both Mme.

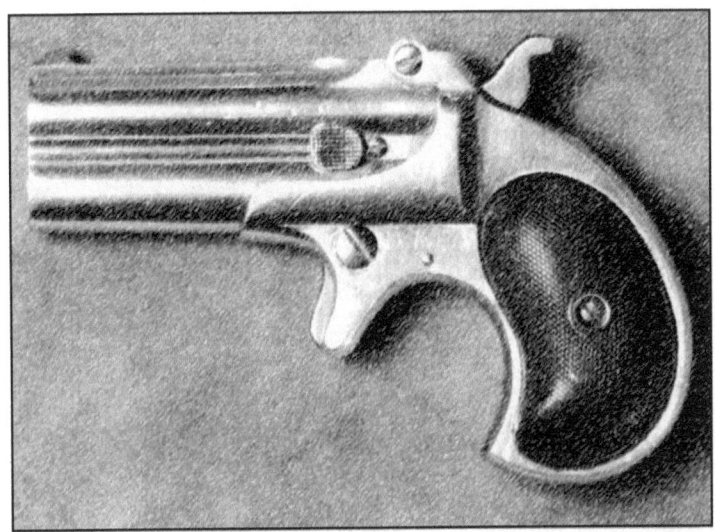

Remington double derringer

Galienda and Mrs. Taylor, who were close friends, said they fired their pistols when they jointly visited a rifle and small arms range on Staten Island "as they desired to learn how to shoot properly."

Miss Henshaw said she fired hers at a man who tried to enter her Second Avenue apartment by the fire escape. She missed but he fled anyway. Detectives visited the apartment and recovered the bullet from the wall by the window.

A report noted that in his interrogation, Ricci claimed that his derringer was in his violin case that was stolen on March twenty-third, five days before the murder. However, he filed a robbery report the day after the violin was discovered missing, but in the report he did not mention that any pistol was in the case.

—◆—

"Honestly, I didn't have that much interest in Ricci," Mme. Galienda said.

The Metropolitan Opera House

She was sitting with Nolan in the front row of the opera house's nearly empty auditorium after lunch as new violinists were auditioned on stage. As a favor, she and Mrs. Taylor had come in early to accompany the auditioning musicians. Mrs. Taylor was on stage at the moment.

"I liked him and enjoyed his company, but he mistook my kindness to him," Mme. Galienda said. "He thought it meant much more than it did. He would send me flowers when I had featured roles, but the cards he sent with them made me cringe."

"Like what? What would the cards say?"

"My beautiful songbird. My beautiful nightingale. Things like that."

The Metropolitan Opera House, built in 1883,

looked to Nolan like any drab industrial building from the outside, but on the inside, it was elegant and unique. Tier upon tier of boxes and balconies with gold facades rose nearly five stories above the floor seating. And at the center of the ceiling was a massive sunburst chandelier.

For a moment, they both watched Mrs. Taylor on stage with the current violinist. She was singing from sheet music with great soaring notes and arm movements, as if it were an actual performance. Nolan admired opera but, at times, found it nearly comical in its earnestness.

He returned to the notes in his diary. "In the interviews with detectives, several of the women in the company said Mr. Granados flirted with them and they weren't happy about it."

"He was married, so I don't know how seriously anyone took it."

"I'm just reading what one of the women said. Quote. Alfredo would not leave you alone once he got his eye on you. He didn't care that he was married. He seemed to believe he had a right to every woman he found pretty, even to those he didn't find pretty."

He looked over at Mme. Galienda for a response.

"If that's what someone thought, then that's what they thought. But I didn't feel that way."

"So he showed interest in you also."

"I suppose he did. But, as I said, he was married, so I didn't care and I didn't take it seriously."

"How did he express his interest? Did he try to kiss you? Did he force his way into your dressing room? Others said that."

"Nothing like that. He said something once, and I

shook my head and said I wasn't interested, so it ended."

Nolan turned a page in his diary. "Again, in the detective's report, one company member said this. Quote. Celeste had a rough time with him. It drove her to tears. I know because one time she rushed into my dressing room to escape him and was sobbing."

"I ... I think whoever said that got the wrong impression about why I rushed in. But honestly, I don't recall anything like that ever happening."

With Mme. Galienda watching, Nolan wrote in his diary.

"Another question, if you don't mind. Weren't you and Ricci from villages in Italy that were very near each other, just five miles apart?"

"I've never looked on a map to see how close they were, but I guess they were close. So? Many people were from that region. Verona, a city, was just a few miles away. It doesn't mean anything."

"What do you mean you've never looked on a map? If you grew up there, wouldn't you know where a village was that was five miles away?"

"I ... I was a child. I knew nothing of maps." There was annoyance in her voice. She stood and walked to the front of the stage to listen. When the piece was finished, another violinist mounted the stage and Mme. Galienda exchanged places with Mrs. Taylor, who joined Nolan in the front row, sitting several seats away.

Nolan had learned that her husband left her just before Christmas and now she shared an apartment with Mme. Galienda on Central Park West.

As she settled, Mrs. Taylor called back to the stage. "Celeste, let's hear the Verdi again. See if you can sing it as well as I did." They both laughed at that.

Mrs. Taylor was English, Nolan realized. While singing, it was impossible to tell that. She was about his age with jet black hair and a blunt nose, but the most noticeable thing about her was her discolored front teeth. He wondered if she wore dentures or tooth caps of some kind during performances.

He moved over to the seat next to her, leaned in, and whispered, "I'm a detective looking into the shooting. If you don't mind, can I ask you some questions?"

"Another detective? ... I suppose so."

Nolan did not identify himself as a private detective, hoping to be mistaken for a police detective. His profession was hated by many.

He reopened his pocket diary. "To start, I've heard Mr. Granados annoyed many of the women in the company by flirting with them. Did he ever bother you that way?"

"I'm married, so no, he didn't."

"Aren't you and your husband separated, though? I heard you share a flat with Mme. Galienda."

"I have for the last few months. But I'm still married."

"And Mr. Granados never bothered you in the manner we're talking about?"

She turned and eyed him, as if trying to figure what lay behind the question. "You asked if he bothered me. No. Did he flirt with me? Yes. He did with every woman. But as I said, I'm married."

"Then let me ask about the pistol you owned. You and Mme. Galienda both bought Remington pistols. Is that correct?"

"Yes, the derringers. Then Celeste – Mme. Galienda – took me to a shooting range she knew about so I could learn to fire it. She had some experience with pistols already. I told all this to the other detective. That's why mine was fired in the last two weeks."

"And Mme. Galienda fired hers there also. Is that correct?"

"Yes, she did."

"And you're sure of this?"

"Of course, I'm sure."

"You saw her fire it, saw the pistol jump in her hand?"

Mrs. Taylor looked over at him with irritation. "I said I did, so I did."

"I spoke to the man at the firing range who said only one of you women fired that day, that the range was crowded and only one stall was open."

She paused only a second. "Celeste and I took turns. Did your man watch us the entire time? Of course not, so he didn't see us change places. Go back and ask him about that, why don't you."

"I will, Mrs. Taylor."

She turned to him, glaring. "What are you accusing me of?"

Nolan decided to confront her with the implication to see what response he got. "All the derringers were fired recently, but if one of you women did not shoot your derringer at the range that day, perhaps that was the person who shot Mr. Granados."

"That's ridiculous. Ricci shot Alfredo."

"And how do you know that?"

"Everyone knows that. He's in jail, for God's sake. What's the point of this?"

"Maybe Ricci didn't shoot him. Maybe someone else did. Others bought these derringers too."

"Are you talking to them?"

"Besides you and Mme. Galienda and Ricci, only one other person bought one. Miss Henshaw."

"Then you should talk to her also and you should be insulting her with accusations also, if that's how you conduct yourself. You won't have any trouble finding things to ask that girl if you have suspicions. She's no saint."

"What would you propose that I ask her?"

She thought about this a moment. "Ask her how she suddenly got raised from the chorus to understudy to the great Geraldine Farrar when others of us are so much more deserving."

"Who is Geraldine Farrar and I apologize for my ignorance of your profession."

"Farrar is Farrar, the greatest soprano perhaps ever. You *should* apologize for not knowing about her. In fact, you should apologize for never having heard her, which I assume you haven't, being the kind of person you are."

Nolan let her comment pass. "And how did Miss Henshaw get named her understudy?"

"Sometimes, it's who you know," Mrs. Taylor said.

"And who did she know?"

She thought a moment before answering. "There was a rumor it's a man on the board of directors. Someone saw them twice at late night dinners at the Hotel Astor. So you should ask Miss Henshaw about that, why don't you."

Then she rose and walked out of the auditorium.

As the auditions continued, Nolan found the assistant stage manager in the wings and told him he was part of the defense team for Ricci. A rough-looking man, he had an Italian accent.

"If you're working for Mr. Ricci, I'll help however I can. He was always kind to me. You can't say that about many of these performers."

"What did you know about the dead man, Granados?"

"Not a likable fellow. The women, especially, had their problems with him."

"What did you hear?"

"He went after them like an alley cat, trying to get them into his bed. I heard he would ask around if there were any rumors about the women he had his eye on to —"

"You mean scandalous things about them."

"Yes. He even came to me one time and asked if I knew anything about Clara – Mrs. Taylor. He winked at me, and said, 'Maybe I can use it to convince her.' I said 'convince her of what?' He said, 'you know,' and he winked again. I didn't like the man at all."

Nolan took notes in his diary. "What can you tell me about Fredericka Henshaw?"

"Oh goodness, an adorable girl and the nicest singer in the company." He said that for most of the time Granados was with the Met, which was less than a year, Miss Henshaw was on a leave of absence. "Just before he started with us, she went upstate. She was tired and needed a rest and there was concern it would affect her voice. So she was granted a six-month leave. She had been back only a month or so when Alfredo was killed."

"Did Mr. Granados ever bother her, as far as you know?"

The assistant stage manager laughed slightly and leaned in confidentially. "One time Alfredo said something to her and grabbed her around the waist. Fredericka is a petite girl and I guess that scared her. But as soon as she got back from her leave, she met a man, a big man, a police officer in the mayor's special police detachment, and in a matter of weeks they were engaged. So when Granados grabbed her that time, she invited her fiancé to come to a rehearsal to have a little talk with him. You can bet it was the last time *that* ever happened."

"One other question, if you don't mind. Mrs. Taylor. I've heard her husband left her. Would you know the reason?"

Again, he laughed slightly and leaned in close. "She told me the story that it was her who left him, that he was having an affair. But I'm pretty sure that she was having her own little affair with one of our stagehands ... I gotta get back to work, friend."

Nolan stayed briefly, standing in the shadows of one of the first-tier private boxes to watch Mme. Galienda and Mrs. Taylor talking between auditions at the edge of the stage. What could he make of their expressions? Were they comparing interviews? Conspiring?

If Ricci did not commit the murder, he was willing to bet one of these women did – but which one? Both had lied to him about something. Why would you lie to a detective investigating something serious like a murder unless you had a reason? Maybe they cooked up this murder together, he thought.

———◆———

That afternoon, he tried to track down the three buyers who had come to Ricci's apartment. All lived in the wealthy neighborhoods around Central Park. He only spoke to one of them, a banker, who, as investments, bought violins, violas, cellos, harps, and other instruments that bore the names of Amati or Stradivari.

"You could have bought a Stradivarius for three thousand dollars ten years ago. Now that same piece would sell for twelve thousand. Tell me where you can get that kind of return on your investment anywhere else," he told Nolan.

The second buyer was an amateur musician but president of the New York Philharmonic Society. And the third was the wife of the former lieutenant governor of New York. These were not people likely to be break-and-enter thieves, he decided.

Next, starting in the midtown region, he went to pawnshops and music shops in search of the Amati. By the time he finished, even he could tell the difference between an expensive, centuries-old, finely crafted violin and one hastily manufactured in New Jersey in the most recent decade. The stolen Amati was not among them.

Over the next day, he widened his search to the rest of Manhattan and beyond, to Long Island, Staten Island, and finally Brooklyn, but with nothing to show for it.

❖

"Mr. Ricci did it, so why should I bother to talk to you?" asked Granados' widow. She would not fully open the front door to Nolan. Their first-floor apartment was in a building on Fifth Avenue opposite the Carnegie mansion.

"I don't think he committed this murder," Nolan said.

"Well, District Attorney Swann, who I spoke to, surely believes he did."

"Did the district attorney tell you three women in the company also bought derringers?"

This puzzled her, but the door did not budge. "No, he didn't."

"Did he tell you that one of those women was especially angered at your husband, that he had made her cry,
she was so angry?"

"No."

"The district attorney has his mind made up about this
and that's why I was hired, to make sure Mr. Ricci is
treated fairly."

She sighed and seemed to reconsider. "To be honest, I
met Mr. Ricci and thought he was one of the nicest people in the company. So I was surprised when he was
arrested. And to be honest, there was something about
Mr. Swann I didn't like, the way he characterized Mr.
Ricci as an Italian. So I'll talk to you because I suppose I
want to see him treated fairly too."

She opened the door and they moved to the front
room, much of which was empty, save for a few larger
pieces of furniture. There were packing boxes along the
wall filled with smaller items – vases, crystal pieces, and
small framed photographs.

They took seats and Nolan asked her introductory
questions. Did her husband express worries about ene-
mies? ("Not that I recall.") Did he mention anyone in
particular in the company who he was having trouble
with? ("He didn't talk about those problems at home.")
Did she notice anything unusual in the letters or telephone calls he received?

"Actually, to that question, yes. Some letters I can't
explain. I found them in his study and practice room. I
was his personal secretary for two years before we married, and I still take in his mail, but I never saw these."

She rose and walked toward the hall, so he followed. It
was difficult not to notice she was only in her twenties,

less than half the age of her husband. Small, thin, and attractive, she had black hair and heavy eye liner that was just as black. Her accent was British.

Nolan knew he had a bad habit of jumping to conclusions, not something a detective should do, but he could not seem to stop himself. With her, his conclusion was that she had been poor when she was Granados' secretary, so she married him for the glamorous life and the wealth it would bring her. He married her to have someone to keep his life organized at home. Whether there was any truth in his theory, he did not know.

However, ever since Nolan came into the apartment, she had been unconsciously wringing her hands, as if washing them with soap. With as many complaints as he had heard about her husband's philandering, he expected his widow knew about them too and would be less distraught about his death than she was. However, she seemed genuinely upset, close to tears in fact, as if she had truly been in love with him.

The study was a museum devoted to the musician. Along with the framed commendations and awards covering the walls, there were framed photographs with inscriptions showing Granados posing with famous people. Enrico Caruso, Lloyd George, Charlie Chaplin, Theda Bara. If there was wallpaper on the walls, it would have been hard to find.

Oddly, there were no musical instruments to be seen. Another assumption. A famous musician would have an expensive violin that he would lock away because of its value. And yes, there was a large black safe in the corner of the room. Nolan wondered if there was a way to look inside. Would he find the Amati? Could Granados have hated Ricci enough to have stolen his treasured violin?

"Excuse all the boxes," she said, opening the desk drawer. "I've got to move. There's no more income." With this, she sobbed one great sob, a huge gulp of air, as if the wind had been knocked out of her. Then she composed herself as she pulled out a stack of letters, tied with a string.

"These letters – I found them while packing. He had them sent to a post office box and not here. I don't know why. The postmarks say they came in the last three months."

He handed Nolan the envelopes then sat at her husband's leather desk chair.

The envelopes all had return addresses from various cities and towns in Missouri – Blue Springs, St. Louis, Ballwin, Independence. And they were sent by various boards and departments – Office of Vital Records, Office of the Registrar, Department of Health. The thickest envelope, which Nolan opened first, was sent from the St. Joseph Board of Registrars.

Along with a letter, it contained a folded sheet. A certified copy of a birth certificate. Agnes Adeline Williams, born at home on May ninth, 1871, at 914 Mitchell Avenue.

The letter with it was short. "Dear Mr. Granados. Your wired payment was received. I hope this is what you sought. Sincerely, Alton F. Richards, assistant registrar."

The other envelopes contained letters saying no birth record for an Agnes Williams could be found in those towns around the date given.

"And you have no idea what this is about?"

"None. Alfredo was from Spain. Why would he be looking for the birth certificate of someone from

Missouri? And this name, Agnes Williams – I've never heard it."

Nolan made notes in his diary and returned the letters to her. "Let me ask you again. Did he ever say anything about, well, about arguments with women in the company, about disagreements?"

She sighed. "Alfredo could be a difficult person and ... he ..." She had to pause. Her eyes were tearing and her mouth trembling.

Suddenly, Nolan was swept with compassion for her and touched by her despair. "You miss him, don't you." He reached over to put a hand on hers, but she bolted out of the chair before he could.

"Miss him? God, no. My life is a nightmare! And it's his damn fault!" she said as she began pacing the floor. "Every day I wake up and realize what's happened to me and I can't believe it. I had this apartment, this life. We had friends in society. Now? Nothing! I have nothing! In one second, it was all gone. And these friends we had, now that he's dead, they won't even talk to me. It's like I've got a disease."

She paused only briefly to wipe her eyes with her sleeve.

"My husband never thought of me! He was selfish! A selfish bastard! He never bothered to buy life insurance. You know why? Here's how that bastard thought. Why spend my money now for something I'll never get, money that will go to someone else. So instead he spent every penny he made on the best wines and cigars, on expensive evening clothes and God knows what else. Yesterday, I went to see how much we have in the bank, and the accounts are barely enough for next month's rent. Oh

God! Oh my dear God!"

She sat and broke down, crying without restraint, giving in to it completely.

Nolan could only stand by and quietly wait for it to end. When it did, as he was about to leave, he asked if her husband's violin was in the safe. Maybe that was worth a great deal, he said.

"I don't know," she said. "I don't have the combination. My husband never got around to giving it to me. But the locksmith who sold it to him is coming tomorrow afternoon and he's got it."

"Would you mind if I come back to see it opened? Maybe there's an explanation for these letters in it." What he really wanted to look for was Ricci's Amati.

"I don't give a damn. Do anything you want. Lock the door on your way out."

⟡

In the Criminal Courts Building, the district attorney, Edward Swann, tall, graying, and fit, rushed out of his office and past Nolan who was sitting in the waiting room with half a dozen other people.

"Sorry, no time to talk," Swann said as he passed. "Have to get to court downstairs."

Nolan decided to follow him. In fact, Swann left the building. It was nearly noon and lunch was the more probable destination, he figured.

Sure enough, Swann walked to a saloon nearby on Centre Street. A buffet of roast beef, pickled pigs feet, cheese, and rye bread was laid out on the bar. Swann had the bartender draw him a beer as he filled his plate.

Nolan had done some research on Swann. Put up for office by the corrupt Tammany Hall ring, he had been dis-

trict attorney since 1915, but he was investigated several
times for misconduct since, including trying to intimidate a
witness against him in one of the investigations.

Nolan approached the bar, started a plate for himself,
then looked over as if just recognizing Swann. "Sir,
you're attorney Swann, aren't you? Coincidentally, I'm a
private detective asked to work on a case that you've got,
the Metropolitan Opera murder."

"So what?" Swann did not even glance over, apparently
used to being accosted in the court district by lawyers,
defendants, and others.

"I just thought you'd like to know what I found. Maybe
it's things your men didn't."

Swann thought a second and apparently saw the self-
interest in talking to Nolan.

"Then get your meal and join me," he said, picking up
his plate, the beer, and a small bowl of pickle relish. "I'll
be at a back table."

The smoky saloon was starting to crowd with men
there for the lunch buffet. Tables went quickly. Swann
was already devouring his sandwich as Nolan sat.

"Who hired you?" he asked.

"I'm working for an attorney the board of directors of
the Metropolitan brought in."

"Attorney for whom?"

"For Mr. Ricci."

Swann snickered and wiped mustard off his mustache.
"Then they're throwing away their money. Everything
points to this Dago."

"I found a few things that didn't. The dead man,
Granados, was hated by a lot of women in that opera
company because he hounded them for sex. And they

bought derringers too."

"So your theory is a woman shot him?" His tone was derisive.

"Women do that, sir. They shoot people too."

"Not in this case. Ricci's is the only derringer that went missing. Very convenient."

"It was in his violin case and that got stolen a few days before."

"Again, very convenient. Just says he planned this in advance."

"I talked to two of the women whose pistols had recently been fired and in those interviews both lied to me about one thing or another."

"So? Women lying. Is that something new?"

"When it's a murder investigation and they're lying to a —"

Swann waved his hand. "Doesn't matter. This man Ricci was witnessed arguing with the deceased just before the shooting, and the first thing he said to the detectives who went to arrest him was 'is the man dead?'"

"I think he said 'is someone dead?' He thought they'd come to the Metropolitan to tell him that a relative had died."

"That's not what the detectives say."

"I read the detective's reports, sir. If they'd heard Ricci say 'is the man dead?' it would have been in the reports."

"It was close enough. It's what a jury will believe Ricci meant."

"You mean it's what you'll try to convince them he meant."

Swann turned slowly and glared at him. "You got anything else of interest, detective?"

Nolan hesitated only a moment before a boldness over-took him. "Yes. My intuition. It says Ricci didn't do it."

Swann laughed. Then he pretended to take a pen from his pocket and write on his napkin.

"The Irishman said the Italian didn't do it because his intuition tells him so. All right. I've got that down. Case settled. Release the prisoner."

"If there are other possible suspects, shouldn't —"

"This man Ricci did it and that's all there is to it. I want this conviction. It makes people angry when important people get murdered in this city. And it makes them mad that Italians are doing so much of the mur-dering these days. It makes people feel like no one's safe. So you and your intuition go sit someplace else, Mick. I'm eating."

The locksmith checked the slip of paper in his hand and twisted the dial to the right, then the left. He grabbed the safe handle and gave it a big pull. The heavy iron door swung open and he backed away. A violin case was immediately visible. Nolan glanced at Granados' wife who, oddly, made no move to retrieve it, so he stepped forward.

"I've been looking at violins lately. I can tell you what you've got here."

He opened the case and first looked for the sewn-in bag containing the derringer. There was none. With great care, he lifted the violin out and carried it to a window where the light was better. Peering in the F-hole, he locat-ed the label. All of the label was perfectly visible. And the name on it was not Amati: It was Stradivarius. "Antonius Stradivarius Cremonensis Faciebat Anno 1732."

The violin safe

"It's your husband's violin," Nolan said. "It looks like it's a Stradivarius, so you have something very valuable here."

He placed it back in the case and handed it to her. With a vacant look in her eyes, she seemed almost indifferent.

"I've heard they sell for up to ten thousand dollars," Nolan said. "Five to ten thousand."

"At least I'll have something. But how long will it last? I certainly can't live like this anymore." Frowning, she turned to get her purse to pay the locksmith.

Nolan examined the rest of the safe. There was little else in it. It seemed to be intended solely to hold the instrument. However, as he was about to close the door, he leaned farther down and spotted a small drawer near the top of the safe. Opening it, he saw a life insurance policy on top of a stack of documents. It read, "Insurance on the life of Alfredo Granados."

"Mrs. Granados! Life insurance!" He held up the policy, waving it like a flag.

"Really? Oh my God!" She rushed over and took it. "This is wonderful! Alfredo, you dear. You wonderful dear."

She began to read it and make comments as Nolan looked through the stack of other papers that had been in the drawer.

"The Commercial Union Assurance Company. Offices in London and Cornhill," she said.

Nolan found a receipt for two-tone boots from Hogg & Selcher on Fifth Avenue. A receipt for a tuxedo from Hogg & Selcher. Receipts for calfskin gloves and silk handkerchiefs from Hogg & Selcher.

"Oh my Lord! One hundred thousand pounds! A pound is what? Four dollars and something? This is worth more than four hundred thousand dollars. Alfredo! You darling, darling man!"

Then Nolan found an envelope holding a yellowing newspaper clipping near the bottom of the stack. *The London Daily News.* July nineteenth, 1908. "Granados Acquitted" was the headline. He carefully put the brittle paper back in the envelope then into his pocket with the promise to himself to return it later.

Mrs. Granados continued to read through the pages, murmuring pleasant things about her husband as she did. Then, abruptly, the murmuring stopped. Nolan turned. Her expression had hardened.

"Mrs. Granados?"

"I'm not the beneficiary. My name isn't anywhere ... It's his first wife ... and his daughter ... But not me. The policy is for them."

She closed her eyes and gritted her teeth. "Damn," she said in the quietest of whispers. "Damn that man."

—◆—

Nolan waited until he was home that evening to look at the British news clipping, putting it next to an electric lamp on the kitchen table.

GRANADOS ACQUITTED

*Indication from jury
that case lacked evidence*

Jeers in court at verdict

*Mr. Granados and family
drive away quietly*

After an absence of just over an hour, the jury in the Granados case at Central Criminal Court returned a verdict of "not guilty."

Jeers could be heard throughout the room when the finding was read.

The Lord Chief Justice proclaimed, "Mr. Granados, you are discharged."

Alfredo Granados, a violinist this season with the London Symphony Orchestra, had been charged with blackmailing Mrs. James S. Acton, a married female assistant to the orchestra's secretary, concerning an affair he claimed she had entered into with a clarinetist, Thomas Forbes Todd.

Although a letter from Mr. Granados to the woman seemed to indicate the truth of the charges, it was written in a clever enough manner to allow various interpretations.

Mrs. Acton claimed Mr. Granados was demanding that, for his silence, she accompany him to a hotel room for an afternoon, the time to be used at his pleasure.

Throughout the sensational nine-day trial, which offered an intimate view of the private lives of London's celebrated musicians, the wife of the accused sat stoically behind her husband, sometimes bringing their young daughter to the court.

After the verdict was rendered, the Granados family

**quickly departed, taking a
hired motor to an unknown
location.**

Sheenagh came in from the bedroom. "What've you
got there?"

"Something from the Granados' safe, a news article.
He was on trial in London in —"

"Who was on trial? Ricci?"

"No, the dead man. The trial was a decade ago. He
was accused of blackmailing a woman who worked for
his orchestra for sex. He was acquitted."

"So what does that tell you?"

"He might have been doing the same thing at the
Metropolitan. But to who?"

"You're the only one who bought a derringer who I
haven't interviewed," Nolan said.

"You've talked to Celeste and Clara?"

Nolan nodded. They were in Fredericka Henshaw's
temporary dressing room above the Met's main stage.
Wearing a black wig and a bathrobe, she was using a tiny
paint brush to apply heavy black lines around her eyes for
that evening's performance of *Carmen*.

The dressing room was usually Geraldine Farrar's, but
the renowned soprano had a cold and was expected to
miss that night's performance. As Farrar's understudy, she
had been asked to step in. It would mark the first featured
role that she had ever sung at the Met.

"I'll tell you what I can," she said as she studied herself
in the makeup mirror. "But I didn't know Alfredo at all. I
was on hiatus when he started with the Met."

"I was told you took a six-month leave in upstate New York to rest your voice."

"In Oswego."

"What was in Oswego?"

"Just a hotel on Lake Ontario. It was very restful, very scenic. I've been singing for the Metropolitan for two years. I don't know what you know about opera but a mezzo-soprano can be a very busy singer, even in the chorus."

She was momentarily silent. Nolan watched her apply ruby-red lip coloring and more black shading above and below her eyes for the role of the gypsy beauty.

"You know, from the audience, the makeup doesn't look as heavy as it does close up," he said.

"That's the point. To look natural even from the balcony. But close up, no. It can look hideous."

"So this must be quite a night for you."

She nodded, her nervousness evident. "The most important night of my life. You know who sings Don José opposite me? Caruso. Enrico Caruso. I can't believe it myself. To be named understudy to Farrar, one of the greatest voices you may ever hear, that was enough, but now to sing in her place – it's … it's inexpressible."

A second paint brush began to roll on the table and Nolan put his derby down to stop it. She looked at him in her mirror.

"You know, with your hat off, you look quite a bit like George Kiefer, the stage actor."

Nolan shrugged uncomfortably.

She smiled. "Don't be shy about it. He's quite a handsome fellow. I've met him."

"I understand you're engaged now," Nolan said, trying

to change the subject.

"Yes, to a man in your profession, a police officer. A wonderful man. I have a sister who died in childbirth earlier this year and he's agreed to adopt her baby. He's on his way here now, if you'd like to wait and meet him."

"I might. Another question. It seems to be common knowledge that Mr. Granados made unwanted advances to many women in the company."

"Women in the company, women in the audience, women on the street, women in —"

"Did he ever approach you?"

"Not really."

"What does 'not really' mean?"

She apparently saw his suspicion in the mirror. "He did once. But nothing happened."

"How did you respond?"

"I didn't. I walked away."

"Did he say something? Did he touch you?"

"He said something and I walked away."

"He didn't grab you around the waist."

She glanced at him in the mirror as she applied red blush to her cheeks. "So you've heard this story, have you. Yes, my fiancé came down the next day and talked to Granados, you might say forcefully, and that was the last rude thing he ever said to me."

He felt the need for boldness. "What's your opinion in the case? Did Mr. Ricci kill Mr. Granados."

She put down the brush and turned to him. "Actually … no. No, I don't. I like Ricci very much. He was always so kind to me, so courteous. I can't imagine him picking up a gun and shooting someone for any reason, so I don't understand this at all and I'm glad they've hired someone to help him." She stood now. "If you don't mind. I have to get dressed."

There was a knock on the door behind them. It was the Met's stage manager. "Farrar is here and will sing. You'll have to give up the dressing room." Abruptly, he turned and left.

Instantly, Miss Henshaw dissolved into tears. Black streaks quickly formed on her cheeks. She turned to Nolan. "Please leave."

In the hallway, Nolan waited for the tiny wooden elevator that was just coming up from the stage wings. Through the open grillwork, he saw a man reading a newspaper in it. Nolan waited for him to exit. In his forties perhaps. Big like a policeman. Brusque and impassive like a policeman. Heavy black shoes like a policeman.

To Nolan, he was not the fiancé that such a young, pretty girl would be expected to have.

The man passed and Nolan waited a moment to see where he was going.

He stopped at Miss Henshaw's door and knocked.

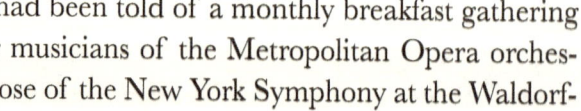

Nolan had been told of a monthly breakfast gathering of former musicians of the Metropolitan Opera orchestra and those of the New York Symphony at the Waldorf-Astoria in Manhattan. They convened on the first Saturday of every month.

He got there early and, after identifying himself as a detective, asked those who came in if anyone knew Granados well enough to answer some questions about him. He got little response until he thought to mention he was working for Ricci's defense. Then men spoke to him without hesitation.

"I worked with Granados in London," said an elderly man who walked with the support of two canes.

"Then you might have heard about charges brought against him there for —"

"For blackmailing a woman. Yes. I played with him in Heidelberg too, and the same charges were about to be brought against him there, but he got out of Germany before they were filed. A shame."

"I have suspicions he was doing the same thing in New York," Nolan said.

"That's what I heard from friends at the Met. It's no secret."

Nolan asked another man, a trumpet player, if he had heard the blackmail rumors. He had not.

"But then again, I only know one performer still at the Met and I haven't seen her in years. Mme. Galienda. I worked with her twenty-five years ago, during her early days in musical theatre in stock companies in New York. She wasn't madame anything in those days."

"In New York? I thought she began her career in Europe, that she trained to sing opera there," Nolan said.

"When I worked with her – and this was in 1893 – she'd just gotten married. Her husband's name was Galienda. I don't recall her maiden name. But I don't recall her having a foreign accent. Sounded American to me, the few times I heard her speak. But maybe she was born in Italy and came here as a child. I know a lot of people in opera, and in the theatre, exaggerate on their resumes, though. This idea she was European – maybe that was one of those little white lies to make herself look more important in the opera world."

"Can you remember anything else about her?"

"I only played for her. I don't believe I ever spoke to her in a personal way. She was in her early twenties at the time, and I do remember she had the most wonderful raw, powerful voice but completely untrained. It was something to hear and you knew she would one day be someone. I don't know how much opera training she'd had, if any at all. I guess they moved to Europe after New York and she got the training she needed there. That's where she made her name in opera before she came back."

"Are you sure about this, that she began in New York?"

"Yes. I played for her in *The Spice in the Sauce*, a musical revue at the Casino Theatre that ran nearly five months."

"Are you sure you can't remember her maiden name?"

"I don't, but here." He drew an address book from an inside jacket pocket and began to search through it. "You can write a friend of mine. He's retired in Florida, but he knew her for several years before her marriage. He was the road manager for the stock company she was with. He'd remember."

He found the entry and turned the book toward Nolan, who wrote down the name and address in his diary.

Theodore Myers
11 Lime Street
St. Augustine, Florida

—◆—

Nolan learned the charges came back from the grand jury. First-degree murder.

Sheenagh went with him to the Tombs to console Ricci. When Ricci was brought into the visitor's room, he appeared more forlorn, more despondent, than he had in any of their visits. Nolan glanced at Sheenagh. She looked like she might break into tears.

"Please, ask the guards to watch him," she whispered to Nolan. "He might try suicide."

"If you're here because of the trial date being set, I already know," Ricci said as he sat down. "I don't stand a chance."

"Don't think that," Sheenagh said. "There's always hope."

"In your world maybe. Not in mine."

"Ricci, our best bet is to find your violin case and your derringer. I've asked you this before, but did anyone in your building know where you hid it? Any friends? Someone from the orchestra?"

"No. No one ever came to my apartment."

In a spontaneous outpouring, Ricci began to complain about his life in the Tombs, the deplorable conditions, the inadequate meals, the rats and mice, the meanness of the guards. Sensing he badly needed to talk, they did not interrupt, even though their half hour was passing quickly.

The guard finally rapped the table with his nightstick. "Two minutes."

As they rose to leave, Nolan thought of something. "Ricci. The Foster Brothers – you told them you would sell the violin to raise money to invest. Isn't that correct?"

He nodded.

"Did you tell them how much it was worth?"

"I did, but I told them I only would spend a thousand on the stock. I needed the other four thousand to buy a new instrument. I knew of another Amati for that price."

"What was their reaction to that?"

"To what? To my buying another violin?"

"No. To your saying it was worth five thousand dollars."

"Let me recall. I think Louis said, 'Why Ricci, if you buy five thousand dollars of this stock, you can buy ten Amati violins.' I said, 'No, I could only spend a thousand more.'"

"And what did Foster say to that?"

"Nothing. He just shrugged."

"Did he ask you where you kept the violin?"

The guard rapped the table again. "Finish it up here."

"Ricci. Try to recall. Did Foster ask —"

"Let me think. I believe his brother did. He said, 'I hope you keep it in a safe place.' I said that I kept it in a place in my bathroom where no one would think to look for anything valuable. But that's all I said."

"Where else in your bathroom could you have hidden a violin case, other than the laundry hamper?"

He thought a second. "I guess nowhere."

"I was told to see the publicity man," Nolan said. He was standing in the door of the business office of the Metropolitan.

"He's not here at the moment." The young woman had said she was the "sitting-in" secretary during the lunch hour. "Can I ask what's it about?"

Nolan showed his badge quickly in hopes she would think he was a police detective. "I'm looking for your publicity files on a few women in your chorus. I'm trying to find out something about their backgrounds."

She reached for a file cabinet and drew out a folder. "We ask our artists to fill these out when they start with us, for purposes of publicity. It's their biography sheet. I don't imagine anyone would object to your looking through them. But you have to read them here."

Nolan tried not to show his excitement. He sat at the empty desk beside the woman and sorted through the pages for the females, quickly finding what he was looking for.

Name: Mme. Celeste Galienda

Maiden   name   if   married: Giordano

Born: Soave, Italy

It said her parents were killed in a ferryboat accident when she was in her twenties and that her one brother, a former policeman, was deceased.

According to her sheet, Clara Taylor, born Clara Hawkins, trained with English soprano Emma White in London before joining the Met. Her two brothers were killed in the Battle of the Somme in 1916.

Frederica Henshaw was born in Oswego, New York, and trained with the American Grand Opera Company of Cleveland before joining the Met. She had one sister – or did at the time of the writing – and her mother and father resided in Arizona.

Looking quickly through all the sheets, more than one hundred of them, he found that in the space provided only Mme. Galienda failed to give any details of her dramatic or musical training while young.

"Who's the leading candidate right now?" Sheenagh asked. She was mashing potatoes for their daughter and watching the bluefish cook in the frying pan.

Nolan was sitting at the kitchen table, sipping from a bottle of Knickerbocker beer and reading through pages of his nearly full diary, trying to interpret the evidence.

"The three women who also owned derringers are obviously the chief candidates, but derringers are not uncommon and it could have been someone else, maybe someone Granados wronged in the past."

"The three women – present the arguments to me for each, as a lawyer would in court," Sheenagh said.

He organized his thoughts. "Well, there's certainly a case for each. The victim, Granados, preyed on women by threatening to expose their secrets. And from what I've learned, there are secrets everywhere in this opera company."

"Why didn't he just hire a brasser off the street?"

"Fear of disease maybe. Or maybe he just liked the challenge his method presented."

"The three women – start with the woman that Ricci —"

"That he was interested in? Mme. Galienda. She's lying about her background. I'm sure of that. She seemed to know nothing about the town in Italy she said she was from, and there's a rumor she began in musical theatre in New York, not in opera companies in Europe, as she tells everyone. Maybe this is what Granados had on her. Then there's her friend, Mrs. Taylor."

"You told me she's not very attractive. Why would the dead man have hounded her?"

"A good question, but who can figure out what's in the mind of a man like that. However, I found out Mrs. Taylor's been in an affair with an Irish scenery mover at the Metropolitan for more than a year. He's married and she's married. Maybe that's what Granados had on her."

"What about the third woman?"

"Miss Henshaw. She seems to me the least likely. She's the only one who doubts Ricci did it. However, one shouldn't rule out anyone. It turns out, she was also having an affair. Her lover is a married man who's on the Met's board of directors. I found out it's one of the Vanderbilts and he's nearly sixty. However, it seems to have ended and now she's engaged to a policeman and he's agreed to adopt her dead sister's baby."

"Isn't she the one you told me went upstate to rest her voice?"

"Yes."

"And you believed that?"

"Believed what?"

"That she only wanted to rest her voice."

"Why wouldn't I?"

"John, unmarried women of that age go upstate for a reason."

He waited for the explanation.

"To have a baby," she finally said.

"So you think it's her baby this policeman is adopting."

"I'm not saying it is, but I'm surprised you took her word for that."

He realized he *had* taken her word for it. Was it because she flirted with him and he momentarily forgot his duty as a detective? He sighed at the chance it was true. "You're right, dear. I'll check it."

"And what about Ricci," she said. "Is there any argument to be made against him? Maybe he was lying to us all along, as much as I don't want to believe it."

"Yes, there's an argument, and the district attorney will try his hardest to make it. But my feeling is Ricci lacks the … the streak of dishonesty needed to lie convincingly to us or anyone else."

"I don't think he could either."

"Any mail?"

"On the sideboard. A postcard with almost nothing on it."

"Not even a name?" he asked as he rose from the table.

"Something about a woman. How do you know a woman in Florida? Should I be worried?"

"You should never worry, dear. And I don't know a woman in Florida."

In the front room, he took the postcard out of the pile of mail and knew instantly what it was. "Greetings from the Land of Sunshine" was emblazoned on the front. The stamp cancellation said St. Augustine, Florida.

He had sent a cable to the retired road manager who had traveled with Mme. Galienda in her early years in New York. Theodore Myers in St. Augustine. Nolan had asked him one thing: do you have any information about Mme. Galienda prior to her marriage, such as her maiden name?

Only a few sentences were written in the message pane on the back.

> **I believe her name was Wilson**
> **but I'm not sure. I know she lived**
> **on W. 40th Street because I lived on**
> **the same block.**

First thing in the morning, he was at the front door of the New York Public Library when it opened. Locating the New York City census books in the reference room, he went through several for the West 40th Street entries before a name jumped out at him in the 1892 book.

NAME.	Sex or Female.	Age.	Color.	In What Country Born.	Citizen or Alien.	Occupation.
Agnes A. Williams	f	21		US	c	Stage Actress
George Lahey	m	50		Ireland	a	Laborer
Dennis Lahey	m	17		Ireland	a	Laborer

Census record

Agnes Adeline Williams. Not Wilson. He knew immediately what this meant. Granados had heard the rumor about Mme. Galienda and had tracked down the truth about her. He had found her birth records from Missouri and likely threatened to reveal them as part of his blackmail scheme.

"She would come in about dinner time, rent a room, and pay with cash," said the front desk clerk at the Belleclaire.

Nolan was there to ask about the Foster Brothers, their investment scheme, and the woman who had worked the swindle with them.

"She used the name Pearl Brown. She was an older woman, fifty maybe, matronly. She might sit in the lobby or have dinner until about seven then she'd go up to her room. Then three men would come in and ask for her room. Two of them were always the same men, but the third was alway someone new."

"And how often did this happen?" Nolan asked, slipping another dime under the clerk's copy of the *New York Herald*.

"They did this three times in a week, then it stopped. The first two times it happened, I didn't think anything of it. But when you see a pattern a third time, you begin to wonder what's going on ... I've got one other thing to tell you about this."

First another dime had to go under the *Herald*.

"She's an actress. I chatted with her once at a slow moment and she mentioned she had a speaking role at the Lyceum earlier in the year in a play called *The Widow's Worries* or *The Widow's Woes* or something like that."

The play was *A Widow's Woes*. The press agent for the Lyceum recalled the actress. Pearl Beecher. He also had an address for her: 106 East 72nd Street.

Nolan took a trolley uptown and found her apartment. She answered the door on first knock.

"Miss Beecher?"

"Who're you?"

"A private detective," Nolan said, showing his badge. "I need to ask you some questions."

"And suppose I don't want to answer."

"Then I'll call the police and that won't end well for you. We're looking for the Foster brothers. And don't tell me you don't know them. I've already talked to the clerk at the Belleclaire."

Dressed in a bathrobe although it was nearly noon, she still had not opened the door fully. Nolan put his foot on the sill so that she would not be able to close it, something she saw. Resignation entered her expression.

"It's simple," she said. "They called me for an acting job and told me what to say. But I didn't know the men they brought to the hotel and what it was about. I played the role and took the money and that was it."

"Where can I find the brothers?"

Seeming to sense that maybe Nolan was not after her,

she grew less defensive. "I got a call from them two days ago. Whatever they're doing, they're doing it from out on Long Island now. I have a telephone number for them, but that's all."

The telephone company's central office on Long Island had the address where the phone was installed a week earlier. It was a rented house in Kew Gardens.

Nolan called Jack Baker, the Brooklyn detective who had gone with him originally to the Belleclaire, and they drove out together with a search warrant. The cottage was in a bungalow colony opposite Maple Grove Cemetery. The front door was open and a suitcase was sitting just inside.

"Coming or going?" Nolan said when one of the brothers bent down to pick up the luggage. The man looked up with a start.

"Still moving in," he said uncertainly.

"Maybe you remember me," Nolan said. "I wanted to invest some money with you a few weeks ago."

The brother, who Nolan recognized as Louis, attempted a smile as if nothing were wrong. "Why yes. We were going to meet at the Belleclaire as I recall. But unfortunately something came up."

"So you're out here on Long Island now."

"We ... yes." He seemed to realize that this was likely danger at his door. "What's this about? We're not working with investors at the moment."

Baker produced his badge and they entered.

"Where's your brother?" Nolan asked.

"He's ... he's in Europe. He won't be back until next month."

"I saw fresh auto tracks in the mud in your front yard," Baker said. "You can't live out here on Long Island without a motor. Your brother took it somewhere and my guess is he'll be back soon. So why don't you sit down while we look around."

Baker produced the warrant, and very quickly, Nolan found what looked like Ricci's violin in a closet in a back bedroom. Taking it to the light of a window, he peered in the F-hole and saw the label with the words "fecit anno 1664" obscured by lacquer. However, the bag sewn into the case did not contain the derringer.

Bringing the case to the front room, he held it up. When he did, Foster, sitting on a sofa, reached into his boot and drew out the derringer, aiming it at Baker, who was standing on the other side of the room.

"I'm not going to jail," Foster said. "This is a two-shot and there's two of you. So believe me, I'll get the better of this. So don't budge an inch. You're right, my brother is on his way here and then we'll never see you two again."

For a moment, neither Nolan nor Baker moved as the staring match went on. They were both a good fifteen feet from Foster. Nolan calculated that the chances Foster would be able to hit either with the tiny derringer were small, given his inexperience with it and the pistol's notoriously stiff trigger.

Periodically, Foster nervously turned to look out the front window for his brother. Nolan glanced at Baker. Any time Foster looked away, Baker's hand would slowly go into his coat, where his holstered revolver was. Nolan's revolver was also beneath his coat in a shoulder holster.

When Foster turned again to the window, Baker dropped to the floor, drawing his revolver, and Nolan dove back up the hallway. Foster fired, but as Nolan guessed would happen, the bullet flew wildly, hitting the far wall, a half dozen feet from either of them.

By this time, Baker was ready to shoot. "You drop that little pistol or you're dead, I promise you."

Seeing his predicament, Foster angrily threw the derringer on the carpet. "Damn stupid toy gun."

Baker retrieved it. "Sit down and we'll wait for your brother. Lots of charges here. Attempted murder of a police officer, stock fraud, breaking and entering, and who knows what else. So get comfortable."

An hour later, after the second brother had arrived home and was taken into custody, they drove the handcuffed pair back to the city, where they were charged and jailed. However, when District Attorney Swann learned Ricci's derringer had been recovered, that it and the Amati violin had been in the possession of the Fosters, he refused to drop the charges and release Ricci.

He told the *World-Telegram* that evening, "There are explanations for this that would still make Mr Ricci the killer. He could have conspired with the Fosters, who he admits were his investment agents, to create this elaborate alibi. Were the violin and derringer actually stolen by them? Or did this Italian shoot Mr. Granados and then hand off the violin and murder weapon to them as part of the alibi? It seems very convenient, if you ask me. So, no. Until we know more, no one is being released."

Nolan read Swann's comments and initially dismissed them as the spiteful words of an ambitious DA who was out to convict Ricci, regardless of the truth, and now had a barricade thrown up in front of him. However, as he mulled the argument over – the idea that Ricci and the

Fosters had conspired to create the alibi of the stolen violin case – he could think of no reason that it was not a possibility. And that worried him.

⟨⟩

The telephone rang just after dawn, startling Nolan awake. However, Sheenagh was already up and she caught it on first bell.

She came to the bedroom door. "It's for you. Tell him please don't call this early again. It wakes all the neighbors."

Nolan stumbled to the front room and picked up the instrument. "Hello?"

"John, it's Jack Baker at the Manhattan Bureau. Sorry to bother you like this, but we've got to catch a train in an hour out of Grand Central."

"A train where?"

Nolan wrote down the information the detective gave him. He also wrote down a sentence on a second piece of paper and went to the kitchen where Sheenagh was starting to crack eggs to make breakfast.

"I've got to leave," he said. "But could you do me a favor? Could you call operator information for Oswego, New York?"

"Take a sweet roll with you at least. What do I ask them?"

"Here. I've written it down."

⟨⟩

Binghamton, New York, was nearly four hours upstate by connecting trains. They arrived before noon and walked to the Swift-Reynolds Paint and Specialty Chemical Company building on Water Street.

Baker was carrying a valise holding all the derringers. "We're meeting a man who's an optics expert. He's taking a train down from Rochester, so we're meeting him halfway. The paint company, where my brother is a vice president, has their own laboratory he's agreed to let us use."

The third-floor chemists' testing room had several microscopes on workbenches. The head chemist was directing men as they placed a large tub of water against a firewall. "Is that everything you need, gentlemen?"

"Tell Mr. Baker thank you."

"Your expert is already here. He's using the convenience down the hall."

Max Poser was a scientist for Bausch & Lomb in Rochester, a manufacturer of eyeglass lenses, microscopes, and other optical products. However, he was an expert in microscopy and had made contributions in firearm forensics.

A few months earlier, he had helped save an innocent man from death row by determining that his revolver could not have fired the bullets that killed his neighbors.

The inside of the barrels of pistols and revolvers have spiraling ridge lines that impart a spin to the exiting bullet to keep it traveling in a straight line. And the pattern of the ridge lines is often distinct in each revolver, leaving its imprint on the bullet, like a fingerprint.

Poser had examined a fatal bullet and a test bullet from the alleged murder weapon side by side under a microscope and observed that the patterns of creases on the two were very different.

The method was still considered experimental, and like most new developments in trial evidence, judges were mistrustful of it.

Max Poser studies the bullets

"We're going to do the same thing here with your four derringers," said Poser when he returned. "Why don't we start with the jailed man's weapon."

Baker handed that pistol to him. Poser, a small man who looked every bit the scientist with his graying Van Dyke beard, fired a bullet into the water tub and retrieved it. Then he put the test bullet and the bullet that had killed Granados under microscopes that were positioned side by side. He leaned over each microscope in turn, going back and forth between them several times.

———◆———

Nolan took the wooden elevator to the dressing rooms above the Metropolitan's stage. It was nearly six o'clock, two hours before the curtain for that evening's performance.

One of the larger rooms was being used by several in

the chorus. The door was open and Nolan peeked in. Fredericka Henshaw and one other woman were seated in bathrobes before mirrors, applying makeup.

Miss Henshaw saw him in her mirror and smiled. "Why, it's the actor detective. Joan, doesn't this man look like George Kiefer? Shouldn't he be on stage with us? Sir, what would you like to know?"

"I'm waiting for someone. I'll wait out here."

"Come in. No one's indecent ... yet."

As he entered the room, the other woman left, smiling at him as she passed.

"Mrs. Taylor and Mme. Galienda are a bit late. They room together, you know. They probably couldn't get a taxi right away. By the way, I heard Ricci's trial will still go on next month even though they found his pistol."

"Yes."

"A sorry situation."

"What's the opera tonight?"

"*Faust.* Mine's just a chorus role. A peasant girl."

"How's your voice lately?"

"Excellent. The rest did me well."

"You went to Oswego, if I recall. Didn't I read that you grew up in Oswego, you and your sister?"

She did not immediately answer. She was attaching a false eyelash, applying theatrical glue.

"In fact, didn't you tell me your sister died in child-birth?"

She stopped to study herself in the mirror, glancing at Nolan in the mirror as well. "... Yes."

"Your one sister. Helen Henshaw."

She did not respond, pressing the eyelash into place. He was surprised how unchanged her expression remained.

"Isn't she your one sister? Helen Henshaw?"

"Who are you waiting for? Clara or Celeste?"

"Neither. I'm waiting for a police detective."

"Why?"

"I spoke to your sister a half hour ago on the telephone at her home in Oswego. The baby you talk about adopting is actually yours, isn't it? That's why you went upstate. To have the baby. This policeman who's marrying you – does he know that?"

Her face turned ashen, and her voice fell to nearly a whisper. "No."

"Granados knew, though, didn't he? He knew a member of the board of directors at the Met was likely the father too, didn't he? My guess is that board member arranged for your leave of absence."

Making no move, she stared at Nolan in her mirror. Now an icy calm entered her expression, as if she resolved to show him nothing more.

"Did Mr. Granados threaten to tell your fiancé all this unless you … well, unless you gave in to him?"

Again not answering, she removed the one false eyelash she had managed to attach, then put the jars of creams before her in a careful order, small to large. He still saw no fear or distress in her face, only the same unruffled calm. The ultimate actress, he thought.

"We matched the bullet that killed Granados to your derringer this morning using a new test," Nolan said. "The detective I'm waiting for will have an arrest warrant for you … You know, a jury would have found your story very sympathetic. You might not have gone to prison. But you were ready to let poor Mr. Ricci go to jail in your place. They won't find that sympathetic."

Miss Henshaw reached for a cloth, dipped it into cold cream, and began wiping away the black liner from around her eyes. "I did what I thought I had to do ... Will you wait for me to take off this makeup? I'll look ridiculous at the jail."

"Go ahead. I'll wait."

THE END

About the author

Stan Freeman is a former journalist whose articles have appeared in more than two dozen newspapers, including the *San Francisco Chronicle, Seattle Times, New Orleans Times-Picayune, Houston Chronicle* and *St. Louis Post-Dispatch*. He spent much of his career as the science and environmental writer for the *Springfield Union-News* and *Sunday Republican* of Massachusetts.

Born in New York City, he studied fiction writing at Cornell University and in the MFA program at University of Massachusetts. He's published several short stories in literary magazines and has held a fiction-writing fellowship from the Massachusetts Council on the Arts and Humanities.

The first book in this series of John Nolan detective novels, *The Dutton Girl*, was published by Coffeetown Press of Seattle in 2018.

He lives in western Massachusetts.

Other fiction by the author

PANTOMIME (A novel, 262 pages, $15.95 in paperback, $4.99 for Kindle) – In the spring of 1911, a group of unemployed stage and vaudeville actors in New York City goes to work for a new film company making one-reelers in a converted milk-processing plant across the Hudson River in New Jersey. To their astonishment, they become some of the earliest stars of moving pictures. The story follows these actors' lives through World War I and the rise of Hollywood in the 1920s. Some go on to great fame and wealth in motion pictures, while others slip into obscurity – and worse.

NINETY MILLION AND CHANGE (a novel, 234 pages, $15.95 in paperback, $4.99 for Kindle)

– A young married couple, struggling to pay their mortgage on two school teachers' salaries, discovers they have the winning ticket in a lottery for nearly ninety million dollars. Quickly, their lives are upended as they learn to deal with suddenly acquired wealth and the challenges, moral and otherwise, of life among the "one percenters." New friends, new experiences, a spectacular mansion, exotic travel, and luxury cars all follow. But in the end, not all the changes that come their way prove to be for the better. And in the end, a stock market crash upends their lives once more.

THE DUTTON GIRL (A novel, 304 pages, $16.95 in paperback, $4.95 for Kindle)

– The first book in the John Nolan detective series. In 1915, Nolan is a poorly paid private detective and a recent immigrant from Ireland who only wants to earn enough money to bring his fiancée over from Ireland. When a rich man's daughter is kidnapped in New York City, he is drawn into the case, coming up against police corruption, the Black Hand, and racist stevedores on the waterfront. And before he uncovers the truth, he must survive a biplane pursuit, a gun battle in the Tenderloin, and finally a deadly chase on the tracks beneath Grand Central Terminal.

THE GOD QUESTION

(A novella, 96 pages $5.25 in paperback on Amazon, $1.39 for Kindle) – A scientific breakthrough at Stanford University produces the first supercomputer with intelligence greater than a human's – far greater. It is also able to think independently, like humans. The software that made it possible is quickly confiscated by the U.S. government when the computer goes online and disrupts the Internet. However, Stephen Kendrick, a computer scientist at Johns Hopkins University, has a backup copy of the program and, working in secret, loads it onto his supercomputer. He then asks it the ultimate question. Is there evidence for God, for a spiritual framework to life? Stunningly, the computer arrives at an answer.

THE JUGGLER

(A novella 88 pages, $5.25 in paperback on Amazon, $1.39 for Kindle) – In the 1930s, an Indiana farmboy, Richard Grenier, teaches himself to juggle. Through long hours of practice, he develops astonishing skills, and almost accidentally sets the record for the most balls ever juggled, ten, a feat witnessed by a Ringling Brothers performer. Unfortunately, Grenier suffers medical problems in the closing days of World War II while in the Navy and is robbed of his ability to juggle. Shattered, he returns home and slowly finds the will to build a new life as extraordinary as the one he lost. The story asks the question: How does someone lose what is essentially their life and muster the will to find a new one?